14221

MO   S

REFERENCE LIBRARY

PRESENTED BY School

DATE 24 June '93

CAMBRIDGE MUSIC HANDBOOKS

Handel: *Messiah*

CAMBRIDGE MUSIC HANDBOOKS

GENERAL EDITOR: Julian Rushton

Cambridge Music Handbooks provide accessible introductions to major musical works, written by the most informed commentators in the field.

With the concert-goer, performer and student in mind, the books present essential information on the historical and musical context, the composition, and the performance and reception history of each work, or group of works, as well as critical discussion of the music.

Other published titles

Bach: Mass in B Minor   JOHN BUTT
Berg: Violin Concerto   ANTHONY POPLE
Haydn: *The Creation*   NICHOLAS TEMPERLEY

Handel: *Messiah*

Donald Burrows

Senior Lecturer in Music
The Open University
Milton Keynes

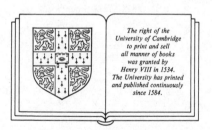

The right of the
University of Cambridge
to print and sell
all manner of books
was granted by
Henry VIII in 1534.
The University has printed
and published continuously
since 1584.

Cambridge University Press

Cambridge
New York   Port Chester
Melbourne   Sydney

Published by the Press Syndicate of the University of Cambridge
The Pitt Building, Trumpington Street, Cambridge CB2 1RP
40 West 20th Street, New York, NY 10011, USA
10 Stamford Road, Oakleigh, Melbourne 3166, Australia

First published 1991

Printed in Great Britain at the University Press, Cambridge

British Library cataloguing in publication data

Burrows, Donald *1945–*
Handel: Messiah.
1. Christian oratorios in English. Handel, George Frideric, 1685–1759
I. Title
782.23092

Library of Congress cataloguing in publication data

Burrows, Donald.
Handel, Messiah/Donald Burrows.
p.   cm. – (Cambridge music handbooks)
Includes bibliographical references and index.
ISBN 0–521–37479–0. – ISBN 0–521–37620–3 (pbk.)
1. Handel. George Frideric, 1685–1759.   Messiah.
I. Title.   II. Series.
ML410.H13895   1991
782.23 dc20   90–2300   CIP

ISBN 0 521 37479 0 hardback
ISBN 0 521 37620 3 paperback

Contents

Contents

Preface

And from that time to the present, this great work has been heard in all parts of the kingdom with increasing reverence and delight; it has fed the hungry, clothed the naked, fostered the orphan, and enriched succeeding managers of the Oratorios, more than any single production in this or any country.

> [Burney, *An Account of the Musical Performances*,
> 'Sketch of the Life of Handel', p. 27]

Charles Burney's assessment of the position that Handel's *Messiah* had gained in the English-speaking world during the forty years since its first performance has been reinforced during the succeeding two centuries. Under modern economic conditions, charities and 'managers' can no longer anticipate automatic profits from performances of *Messiah*, yet the work has retained its hold over performers and audiences, and the oratorio

this are various, related partly to wider musical and social practices and partly to the nature of the work itself. Burney was writing at a moment when *Messiah* was about to take on a new musical guise – or *dis*guise – as a celebratory work for mass performance at the first Handel Commemoration. During the second half of the nineteenth century, when choral singing became a popular movement in Britain, more people came into active contact with *Messiah* than ever before, through large-scale performances in churches and concert halls in London and the provinces. At the same time, small provincial choirs discovered that Handel's music, designed for professional singers to learn on a couple of rehearsals, could be mastered by amateurs in a couple of months. Church and chapel choirs found in *Messiah* a repository of anthems for the ecclesiastical year: in putting Handel's music to such use, they were catching up with an idea that had been familiar in cathedrals since the 1760s.

The continued popularity of *Messiah* can partly be explained by the healthy survival of choral institutions. But only partly. It is still remarkable that a work originally advertised as 'A New Sacred Oratorio' should survive with such vigour through the colder secular atmosphere of the later twentieth century. *Messiah* is at the same time a typical and an unusual Handel oratorio. Typical, in that we can relate most of its musical features to an opera-derived genre in which Handel regularly worked. Unusual, in that the libretto is uncharacteristic of the main run of Handel's oratorios in both its content and its presentation of the story. While the story and its interpretation are matters of religious significance, the tone is not aggressively dogmatic: Handel and Jennens treated their subject as a drama observed and interpreted, as a matter for contemplation. Unbelievers too may appreciate the story and its symbolic interpretation, and ponder on the wider related themes of life and death, providence, sacrifice and resurrection. *Messiah*, like the celebration of Christmas, is sufficiently rich and complex to speak to a range of human needs and emotions, irrespective of its immediate Judaeo-Christian framework.

It is ironic that some of the very qualities that have ensured *Messiah*'s survival were controversial in the years of its first London performances, and even possibly damaging to Handel's immediate professional career. Yet this begs the question of what 'the work' actually is. Performance practices and social changes certainly modify perceptions of such a work: the 'Festival' performances not only altered the sound of *Messiah* into something very different from that heard by Handel's own audiences, but also changed the nature of the piece more subtly by turning it into a 'choral' work. A choral society that rehearses *Messiah*, and then hires an orchestra (or a one-man keyboard substitute) and vocal soloists, is working under artistic premises different from those under which the composer created it. An understanding of the creative process behind *Messiah* requires us to look at the circumstances (themselves changing) in which Handel composed and presented it.

In dealing with the early history of *Messiah*, the writer acknowledges that he himself stands within a historical process. Without the labours of A. H. Mann, Jens Peter Larsen and Watkins Shaw (to mention only the most recent major figures in a 250-year process of scholarly refinement) the materials for my own starting point would have been less tractable. I acknowledge my debt to my predecessors, and count myself fortunate to have been able to discuss *Messiah* topics in person with Watkins Shaw and the late Jens Peter Larsen. For most recent and immediate assistance during the preparation of this book I gratefully acknowledge my debt to Julian Rushton, Anthony Hicks, Ruth Smith, Hildegard Wright and the late Gerald Coke.

References to 'Messiah' editions

Many movements of *Messiah* exist in variant forms composed or adapted by Handel for his own performances. Reference is complicated by the fact that the three principal performing editions in use today number the movements differently. The system of references employed in the left-hand column of the libretto (Appendix 1, pp. 86–100) serves as a guide to the contents of these editions. The three editions are:

B Peters Edition, ed. Donald Burrows, vocal score 1987. This adapts the numbering system from the previous editions by Kurt Soldan (1939) and Soldan/Arnold Schering (1967).

S Novello Edition, ed. Watkins Shaw, vocal score 1959, and subsequent revised reprints. This adapts the numbering system from the previous edition by Ebenezer Prout (1902).

T Bärenreiter Edition, ed. John Tobin, vocal score 1972, derived from Tobin's full score in the Hallische Händel-Ausgabe (Serie I, Band 17, 1965). This edition provided the basis for the movement numbers in the thematic catalogue of Handel's works by Bernd Baselt in W. Eisen and M. Eisen (eds.), *Händel-Handbuch Band 2, Thematisch-systematisches Verzeichnis* (Leipzig, 1984), HWV 56 *Messiah*, pp. 178–97. Where Baselt's designations differ from or supplement *T*, the catalogue numbering is given under 'Comments' preceded by *HHB*.

B and **S** include many variant movements that are not in the preceding editions by Schering/Soldan and Prout, which explains why the numberings of the preceding editions required adaptation. Full scores of all three editions are in print from time to time. One other full score is fairly easily available, edited by Friedrich Chrysander and Max Seiffert for the *Händelgesellschaft* (vol. 45, Berlin, 1902, and several modern reprints). Where it is useful to make reference to this edition, it is called *HG*: it adds no music to that available in **B**, **S** and **T**.

Throughout the book, references to movement numberings are given in the order B/S/T. '–' indicates that the movement or variant concerned is not included in the edition. 'O' indicates a movement included but unnumbered. If a variant is not printed out in full, but is indicated within the text of another variant, the notation 'x' is used (for example, '2x'). All the music of **B** and **T** is included within the covers of their vocal scores, arranged as main text and appendices. In the case of **S**, music in the vocal score (main text and appendix) is supplemented by further movements printed as a Musical Appendix to Watkins Shaw: *A Textual and Historical Companion to Handel's 'Messiah'* (London, 1965): the movements in this appendix are indicated by 'A', followed by the page number of the opening bars. Where particular variant movements are identified as 'versions' in **S**, the following notation is used: '6i' indicates No. 6 version I.

I

The historical background

Messiah was composed within the specific genre of English theatre concert oratorio that Handel himself had developed. Its historical and artistic background can therefore be understood without extended examination of the problems of semantics and categorisation that surround the word 'oratorio'. However, a brief consideraton of the genre is desirable because Handel encountered, and composed music for, various oratorio-type works before embarking on his English theatre oratorios. While any influences from these earlier experiences must have been fully absorbed before he composed *Messiah*, the other traditions may nevertheless have contributed something significant to his decisions about the musical treatment of particular sections. Moreover, the oratorio genre incorporated features that could in certain circumstances produce a conflict between creative expression and social acceptance. In *Messiah*, the artistic and practical issues were focused in their sharpest form, and critically affected the work's initial reception.

Oratorio was created by the application of theatrical musical techniques to a sacred story. While the idea of dramatic presentation of sacred subjects, with or without any musical component, was not new – it was one clear strand of medieval theatre – oratorio itself was a 'twin' creation with opera in Italy at the beginning of the seventeenth century. The first significant landmark, Emilio Cavaliere's *Rappresentatione di Anima, et di Corpo* ('The Representation of the Soul and the Body'), first performed and published in Rome in 1600, was staged and semi-acted in a consecrated building rather than a public theatre; but it was not undertaken within any liturgical framework. The first oratorio merged the forms and techniques of secular entertainment (three acts, continuo-accompanied monody-recitative, choruses and dances) with the circumstances of a devotional exercise.

The subject-matter of subsequent oratorios was quickly broadened to include incidents from the Old Testament, and eventually to embrace subjects from the lives of St John the Baptist or early Christian saints. Oratorio could thus capitalise on the development of musical techniques for the operatic characterisation of 'real' people. As Italian opera moved towards emphasis on solo singing, with extended arias, oratorio ran in parallel. But as opera also became the dominant form of Italian secular theatre, a whole-hearted adoption of a theatrical musical ambience in oratorio brought suspicion or opposition from ecclesiastical authorities.

From motives of puritanical dogma or desire for social and intellectual control, church authorities at various times sought to place restrictions on theatrical performances where they were in a position to do so, and the church's attitude to secular drama was generally uneasy. In Rome, where papal secular control was effective, operas were banned entirely from time to time: when they were allowed, restrictions included a ban on actresses (all female roles were played by men). Where operas were prohibited during the penitential season of Lent, otherwise unemployed musicians could perform oratorios. While the naturalistic representation (within accepted operatic conventions) of biblical or saintly characters in oratorio was generally acceptable, an exception was made for the central figure of Christ, whose impersonation by an actor–singer would have been regarded as offensive, if not blasphemous.

Where any doubt about propriety or ecclesiastical approval was anticipated, oratorio could be distanced from its operatic origins by adopting a concert style without theatrical movement, and sometimes without special costumes or scenery. Inadequate resources could obviously encourage the same trend: oratorios, unlike operas, were presented in a variety of semi-staged and 'unstaged' ways.

Handel in Germany and Italy: passion and oratorio

The more ambitious musical practices of the German Lutheran church in which Handel grew up had adopted from Italian oratorio the principle of applying opera-derived forms of recitative and aria to the setting of religious texts, but on a smaller scale. Zachau, Handel's teacher, composed German church cantatas,[1] but whether they were performed in Halle during Handel's time there is not known: Handel produced no such cantatas as organist of Halle's Calvinist Domkirche. He moved in 1704 to Hamburg, an important centre in the development of extended musical performances of the Passion narrative during Holy Week. In these Passions the German church came closest to Italian oratorio, though they were never staged theatrically and were usually performed within a clear devotional or liturgical framework. It was this non-theatrical presentation that allowed a solo singer to take on the words of Christ in the biblical Passion narrative.[2]

Unfortunately it is not possible to identify the Passion settings that Handel may have heard at Hamburg. Reinhard Keiser's *Der blutige und sterbende Jesus* ('The Bleeding and Dying Jesus') was first produced in 1704, presumably just before Handel's arrival, and the 'St John Passion', formerly attributed to Handel's Hamburg years, is now considered inauthentic. However Handel's *Brockes Passion* ('Der für die Sünde der Welt gemartete und sterbende Jesus', HWV 48), composed in London in around 1716 for performance in Germany, shows that he had a close acquaintance with the genre. Though in a subtly different musical idiom, Handel's treatment of arias, recitatives, choruses and chorales makes an interesting comparison with J. S. Bach's masterpieces of the next decade.[3] His experience of this passion-oratorio genre stood Handel in good stead when he came to set the Passion narrative in Part Two of *Messiah*.

During his period in Italy (1706–10) Handel came into direct contact with Italian oratorio. In Rome, the centre of his professional activity to which he returned between visits to the other cities, opera was currently under a papal ban. For his Roman patrons Handel composed Latin church music, Italian cantatas and two oratorios. The text of the first oratorio, *Il Trionfo del Tempo e del Disinganno* (later translated for English performance as 'The Triumph of Time and Truth') was supplied by Cardinal Pamphili, but little is known of the circumstances of its first performance in 1707. As is clear from the title, this is an allegorical 'morality' oratorio. Much more is known about the circumstances of Handel's second oratorio, *La Resurrezione*, composed for his most constant Roman patron, the Marquis Ruspoli, and first performed on Easter Sunday 1708 as a contrasted companion piece to an Italian passion oratorio by Alessandro Scarlatti, performed the previous Wednesday. The performances took place in a large (secular) room in Ruspoli's Bonelli Palace. Although it was normally forbidden to act oratorios, an elaborate stage setting was erected, including painted backcloths depicting key scenes. The libretto deals with the events between the Crucifixion and the Resurrection. The representation of Christ himself as a participating character is avoided: a dialogue between Lucifer and an Angel culminates with the harrowing of hell, and the events of the Resurrection are dramatised through the discovery of the empty tomb and the appearance of the Angel.

Esther, Handel's first English oratorio

Ten years passed before Handel composed his next oratorio. His career in London revolved around the Italian opera house: it would have needed exceptional prophetic insight to have forseen a musical genre growing from some sort of marriage between Handel's operatic experience and his ceremonial English church music as exemplified by the 'Utrecht' *Te Deum* and *Jubilate* of 1713. Handel's first English oratorio was an accidental consequence of the period between the closure of the Haymarket opera company in 1717 and the establishment of a new permanent opera company, the Royal Academy of Music, in 1719. In the interim, Handel successfully obtained the private patronage of James Brydges, Earl of Carnarvon and subsequently Duke of Chandos. Tantalisingly, just as little is known about the first performance of his first English oratorio as about his first Italian one. On the basis of later secondary testimony, it seems likely that *Esther* was composed for Brydges and performed at one of his residences, probably Cannons, Edgware. Like other works composed for Brydges (*Acis and Galatea* and the 'Chandos' Anthems), *Esther* was probably performed on a chamber scale, with perhaps nine singers and a small orchestra.[4] Handel's title for the work was almost certainly 'The Oratorium',[5] which seems to suggest a generic cross-reference to his earlier Italian oratorios, although the new work was in English. Whether it was acted, with costumes and scenery (or with any of these elements in isolation) is not known.

More than another decade passed before Handel's next venture into oratorio. The route by which he returned to, and eventually developed, English oratorio contains many coincidences and surprises, and certainly did not follow an evolutionary path. In circumstances that are once again tantalisingly obscure, and from motives that are even more so, *Esther* was revived by the Children of the Chapel Royal (presumably with some adult help) under the direction of Bernard Gates, the Master of the Children, in February and March 1732 at the Crown and Anchor Tavern in the Strand. It seems that these performances were staged and acted in theatrical costume, as far as the circumstances of the Tavern's meeting room allowed.

In March 1732 Handel was in the midst of his normal opera season at the Haymarket theatre, but at the end of the season – possibly stimulated by competition from a pirate performance of *Esther*, as well as by the support of those who had seen the recent revival – he took the novel step of performing the oratorio in his opera theatre. This was not, however, a straight transference of Gates's performance onto the public stage. The librettist Samuel Humphreys collaborated with Handel to expand the original six-scene oratorio into a three-act piece of a length comparable to a normal operatic entertainment. The solo parts were taken not by the Chapel Royal boys but by four star singers from Handel's Italian opera company and two English sopranos; the boys, presumably joined by some of the men from the Chapel Royal choir and possibly a few other singers, supported the soloists in the choruses. The performance was not acted, and apparently neither costumes nor decorated scenery were involved.

The intervention of the Bishop of London (who would not permit the Chapel Royal choir to act in the Opera House 'even with books in the children's hands')[6] may be held accountable for this last modification, but its significance can be over-rated. Although the first Italian oratorios were acted in a theatrical style, the alternative path of concert-style presentation was equally legitimate: Handel's *La Resurrezione* was no less an oratorio because it was not staged. More significant was the fact that in 1732 Handel's musical strengths came together into a form of oratorio that suited his time and place. If the new form of *Esther* was unsatisfactory because it inflated the original short work rather more than it could bear, the compensation was that the musical attractions of the operatic style – expert singers and good characterisation – were mixed with those of Handel's grand 'anthem' style, and the whole was in English.[7] Not only was 'the Musick ... disposed after the manner of the Coronation Service', but music from two of Handel's 1727 coronation anthems was worked in. The combination went down well with London's theatre-goers, and there were six well-attended performances. Far from self-consciously creating a new genre for the future with his 1732 *Esther*, Handel seems to have regarded the performances as an extra and varied bonus on the end of his opera season.

1732–1741: from *Esther* to *Messiah*

In the following years, Handel continued to give prime attention to Italian opera, but English oratorio-type works were slipped into his theatre seasons to diversify the programmes, *Esther* being joined by *Deborah* and *Athalia*. Nevertheless oratorio remained peripheral to Handel's main musical programme until the summer of 1738, when two major works –

Saul and *Israel in Egypt* – suddenly claimed his full attention. Compared with its predecessors, *Saul* saw a major advance in musical coherence and dramatic characterisation within the conventions of a non-staged drama. Here Handel worked closely with a new librettist, Charles Jennens, who may also have been responsible for *Israel in Egypt*, an oratorio of a new type: instead of following opera-derived conventions by relying mainly on recitative-dialogue and arias to carry the story-line, the librettist of *Israel in Egypt* took narrative texts from the Bible and arranged them as a succession of choruses, with relatively little solo participation. Here the 'Coronation Anthem' aspect of Handel's oratorio genre was expanded into its ultimate form – too much so, in fact, for contemporary audiences: after the first performance Handel cut down the choruses a little and added some Italian arias.

The new oratorios were first performed in Handel's next season at the King's Theatre, Haymarket during the early months of 1739, together with the English ode *Alexander's Feast* and a revised Italian version of *Il Trionfo del Tempo*. The season ended with the 'Dramatical Composition' *Jupiter in Argos*, an Italian pasticcio, with music derived largely from other works by Handel, and probably only semi-staged. The relative weight of Italian and English works was now entirely reversed: seven years previously, it had been the English works that had come in as the final performances on the end of Italian opera seasons.

1741 marked a decisive break for Handel. The performance of *Deidamia* on 10 February 1741 was the last he ever gave of an Italian opera in London. While Italian opera had hitherto formed the centre of his interests, he had no sympathy with the new management that was seeking to set up a new, high-status Italian opera company.[8] Handel may have foreseen some long-term prospects for his English works in London, though the future appeared uncertain in view of factious divisions among his audiences, which had always been an important concern for his career as a composer-impresario-performer. The success of Handel's operas and oratorios was, for him, measured in terms of the success of the series of performances for which he composed them. Management of performances and performers was Handel's professional concern, no less than composition.

An invitation in 1741 to produce a season at Dublin no doubt came at a welcome time: it gave Handel breathing-space away from London during which he could consider his future, as well as providing him with an opportunity to present his music in congenial circumstances. After his return from Dublin to London in 1742 Handel gave no more operas. His only subsequent compositions in the Italian language were some elegant chamber duets. *Messiah* was composed in the summer of 1741, at exactly this turning-point in Handel's career.

2

From composition to first performance

The composition of *Messiah* took place in a little over three weeks during the summer of 1741. As it came to take its place as one of the 'classic' works within the musical culture of English-speaking communities, the shortness of this composition period was sometimes interpreted as a sign of specific religious inspiration. Handel certainly wrote *Messiah* in an intense burst of activity: even the physical labour of committing the notes to the pages during that period is remarkable.[1] However, the composition of *Messiah* was typical of Handel's normal work pattern: most of his operas and oratorios were written with similar concentration between theatrical seasons. After the completion of a series of performances, Handel naturally turned to the repertory needs of the next.

His method of working resembled that of other composers professionally or temperamentally based in the theatre, such as Mozart or Sullivan. With the libretto already arranged into recitatives, arias and (for oratorios) choruses, the first step was to lay out the whole score, composing the arias and choruses in skeleton draft with the leading voices and instrumental parts, and writing in the recitative texts between the arias. The overall scheme was thereby committed to paper, and the musical shape and tonality of the concerted movements (arias, accompanied recitatives, choruses) established. The hard work went into this 'framing' stage. Handel completed the 'filling-up' of the skeletal outline with composed recitatives and fully-orchestrated movements in two days.[2]

While Handel no doubt used some preliminary musical sketches either before or during the drafting process – though the surviving evidence is small, since most such sketches could immediately be discarded – his real starting-point was literary rather than musical. By 22 August 1741, when Handel began the 'official' composition of *Messiah*, he must have had the libretto to hand. In examining the genesis of the oratorio, the libretto and its compiler–author, Charles Jennens, must receive our first attention.

The librettist

Jennens was fifteen years younger than Handel. He came from a well-connected family with a considerable estate in Warwickshire and Leicestershire, but he had apparently debarred himself from public office, political or ecclesiastical, by a reluctance to take the required oath of allegiance to the House of Hanover.[3] Since the reality of political life in Britain's London-based government was that effective and stable power was in Hanoverian hands, non-jurors such as Jennens felt themselves isolated from the political and social centres of influence. This attitude emerges frequently in Jennens's surviving letters, and especially in the extended correspondence with his friend Edward Holdsworth, who spent considerable periods abroad. From this fortunate circumstance we are able to gain considerable information about Jennens's life and opinions around the period that *Messiah* was composed and first performed.

Jennens's life followed a fairly regular annual rhythm, divided between his family's principal country estate – Gopsal in Leicestershire[4] – and a London house in Queen's Square. He normally spent more than half the year in London, residing there during the winter–spring period between November and May when Parliament was in session. The principal performance seasons in the theatres and the opera house covered the same period, when the largest number of patrons was 'in town'. No doubt the irony of following the social programme of a member of the landed classes without the attendant political influence came home to Jennens most strongly during these months. Yet at the same time, the wealth of cultural activity in London must have been stimulating for him, as he had active interests in painting, architecture, classical antiquity, literature, the theatre and music.[5]

His enthusiasm for Handel's music is apparent throughout the Jennens–Holdsworth letters.[6] Jennens's name appeared in the first published subscription list of Handel's music, for *Rodelinda* in 1725, and evidence of direct contact between them comes ten years later in a letter from Handel, addressed to Jennens at Gopsal:

[GFH to CJ][7]   London July 28 1735

I received your very agreeable Letter with the inclosed Oratorio. I am just going to Tunbridge, yet what I could read of it in haste, gave me a great deal of Satisfaction. I shall have more leisure time there to read it with all the Attention it deserves. There is no certainty of any Scheme for next Season, but it is probable that some thing or other may be done, of which I shall take the Liberty to give you notice, being extreamly obliged to you for the generous Concern you show upon this account. The Opera of Alcina is a writing out and shall be sent according to your Direktion.

From this it is clear that Jennens had put forward a libretto for Handel's consideration three years before their first known collaboration, and that Jennens had already begun to collect manuscript scores of Handel's music by 1735.

Of Jennens's musical literacy there can be no doubt. His attempt at a keyboard-reduction score of *Messiah*, and the extensive basso continuo figurings that he added to his musical scores, are testimony to his desire to convert the scores into practical form, probably so that he could play them through himself.[8] His musical amendments to Handel's autographs of *Saul* and *Belshazzar*,[9] and to the conducting score of *Messiah*, show musical sense and a concern for appropriate textual accentuation, even if his ideas of 'appropriate' did not always coincide with Handel's. Jennens combined practical knowledge of literature and music with an acute critical sense, ideal qualities for collaboration with a composer such as Handel.

Jennens was emotionally committed to the orthodoxy of the Church of England. Institutionally this set him against Dissenters and Romanists alike, and theologically against Quakers and Deists. In common with many non-jurors, Jennens held 'High Church' views which stressed the divinity of Christ: this again tended to set non-jurors apart, as adherents to a partially mystical view of Christianity in a society that was increasingly rationalist. To be an Anglican non-juror in the 1730s and 1740s meant living with an inherent conflict, for while non-jurors could not accept the legitimacy of the Hanoverian succession, neither could they accept the Roman Catholicism of the available Stuart heirs. While the details of Jennens's religious, political and ethical stance may not seem very relevant to the twentieth century, we can nevertheless appreciate the tensions that contributed to his occasional misanthropy.

The collaboration

Such evidence as there is suggests that Handel normally took an active role in his collaborations with oratorio librettists. He changed details of the given texts in various ways during composition, and apparently welcomed the chance to involve himself in the evolution and amendment of oratorio libretti. For other oratorios in which he collaborated with Jennens – *Saul* and *Belshazzar* – there is plentiful evidence of interaction between librettist and composer.[10] Unfortunately there is no comparable direct evidence of any pre-composition collaboration over *Messiah*, and circumstantial evidence suggests that there was no contact between the two during the period that Handel drafted the score. While analogy from the circumstances relating to *Saul* and *Belshazzar* suggests that some preliminary discussion might have taken place, allowance must be made for the fact that *Messiah* has a different type of libretto. Its text, assembled (with various adaptations) directly from the Authorised Version of the Bible, consists principally of short literary units that rarely exceed a couple of biblical verses, and there are no extended passages of conversational recitative. It is possible that there was never any real problem over length, content and declamation where *Messiah* was concerned, and that Handel took Jennens's work as it stood.

The most significant piece of evidence from this pre-composition period comes in a letter from Jennens to Holdsworth:

[CJ to EH]   Gops. Jul. 10. 1741

Handel says he will do nothing next Winter, but I hope I shall perswade him to set another Scripture Collection I have made for him, & perform it for his own Benefit in Passion Week. I hope he will lay out his whole Genius & Skill upon it, that the Composition may excell all his former Compositions, as the Subject excells every other Subject. The Subject is Messiah.

Six extravagant young Gentlemen have subscrib'd 1000£ apiece for the Support of an Opera next Winter. The Chief Castrato is to be Monticelli, the chief Woman Visconti; both of them, I suppose, your Acquaintance.

At first reading, the tone of Jennens's references to Handel might suggest that he had met the composer recently, but the second paragraph seems to be reporting gossip that Jennens had heard before leaving London, and his news of Handel's intentions may also have been at second hand.[11] Handel finished his 1741 theatre season on 8 April: in his letter to Holdsworth of 16 April, Jennens declared his intention to leave London soon, but did not mention a meeting with Handel. Perhaps, during his last days before leaving London, Jennens visited Handel and asked him directly about his plans for the next season. A plausible timetable of events would be that Jennens put the libretto together at Gopsal during May and June and sent it to Handel early in July.[12]

Two details from the letter of 10 July are of particular interest. Jennens refers to *Messiah* as 'another Scripture Collection': the phrase indicates Jennens's awareness that the libretto of *Messiah* was technically different from that of most oratorios, and strengthens the case for Jennens's authorship of *Israel in Egypt*. Jennens's statement that he intended *Messiah* as a work that Handel should perform 'for his own Benefit in Passion Week' is perhaps surprising, both in its content and in the closely specific statement of intention. *Messiah* was clearly intended for performance towards the end of the Lenten season with which oratorios had various historical associations.[13]

August–November 1741: from London to Dublin

Jennens's statement of intention leads naturally to a consideration of Handel's long-term plans when composing *Messiah*. Can Handel's reported statement that he intended not to perform in London next season, and the fact that he left London later in 1741 to mount a season of performances in Dublin, be taken as indicators that he composed *Messiah* specifically for a forthcoming visit to Ireland? Such a supposition seems to receive support from the original scoring of the oratorio, requiring a 'safe' and modest orchestra of trumpets, drums, strings and basso continuo, without even the oboes or bassoons that were regular components of his London theatre orchestra.

Close consideration of the sequence of events during the summer of 1741 suggests a different interpretation. Handel carefully entered the composition dates for *Messiah* into his autograph score: he began on Saturday 22 August, completed the drafts of Part One on Friday 28 August, Part Two on Sunday 6 September, Part Three on Saturday 12 September, and accomplished the 'filling up' of the score on 14 September. After giving himself perhaps a week's break,[14] Handel then began the composition of *Samson*, to a libretto by Newburgh Hamilton after Milton, which he completed in draft on 29 October. The draft score of *Samson* included, in its first stage, an extensive orchestra including flutes, horns and trombones, forces that were currently available in London, from which it appears that Handel was intending to be there for the next season.[15] And, since *Messiah* was composed before *Samson*, it seems most likely that *Messiah* too was composed for performance in London, perhaps for a benefit performance as Jennens had suggested. While the possibility that Handel might have composed *Messiah* for someone else to perform in Dublin cannot be entirely ruled out, it seems very unlikely:[16] the composition of the two oratorios between seasons was entirely typical of Handel's habits when creating a bank of works for his own productions.

Nevertheless, Handel's departure for Dublin followed surprisingly quickly: he was reported as arriving in Dublin on 18 November, less than three weeks after dating the end of Part Three of *Samson*.[17] The all-important questions concerning the timing and background to Handel's decision to go to Dublin must go unanswered for lack of evidence. Some form of official invitation was no doubt received from the Lord Lieutenant of Ireland, but it is inconceivable that Handel would have proceeded without prior negotiations with the managements of the concert-giving venues in Dublin.[18] The most likely interpretation is that a season of performances in Dublin was one of Handel's possible options in the summer of 1741, but his first assumption was that he would remain in London; at some stage, probably during the composition of *Samson*, specific arrangements for a Dublin season were concluded and Handel set up his domestic and professional arrangements accordingly. These arrangements would have included renting a house in Dublin, selecting suitable scores and performing material for the season, and investigating solo singers. Unlike *Messiah*, the score of *Samson* remained in draft stage. From this we may conclude that Handel considered *Samson* too ambitious to be included in his Dublin repertory, and also that arrangements for the Dublin visit had firmed up before he completed the draft of Part Three on 29 October. He did not complete the *Samson* score until he returned to London a year later.

Different as the composition scores of *Samson* and *Messiah* are, they do have one striking similarity. Both were composed to be performable with as few as four soloists, one each in the soprano, alto, tenor and bass clefs. This combination, although fairly standard today, matches no known cast that Handel had worked with during the previous decade, nor any that he employed for the next.[19] His cast at Lincoln's Inn Fields Theatre in the early months of 1741 had included four soprano-register singers but no altos. If Handel was considering proceeding to oratorio performances in London during 1741–2, the outlines of his forthcoming cast were obviously unclear to him. This does not preclude the possibility that the voices and characters of particular London singers might have influenced Handel's musical thinking. The role of Samson, and the tenor-clef part in *Messiah* that carries much of the linking story-line, may have been composed with John Beard in mind: Beard had sung for Handel in many seasons during 1734–40, though he was not in Handel's company during the 1740–1 season. If Handel was preparing for a forthcoming London season when he composed *Messiah*, there were many reasons why he was not ready to book (or even to negotiate with) specific singers: his own plans were uncertain, singers had various contractual commitments to London theatres, and the effects on both performers and audience of Lord Middlesex's prospective new opera company at the Haymarket were impossible to predict.

Arranging singers for Dublin may have been more speculative still: only the soprano Signora Avolio travelled there specifically to take part in his performances. Mrs Cibber, who arrived from London about a fortnight after Handel, joined his company in the course of the Dublin season, but had probably come there initially to perform as an actress at Aungier Street Theatre, which she continued to do after her engagement by Handel. Neither of these women had sung for Handel before, though perhaps he had already 'spotted' them as possible members of his next company before the Dublin visit became part of his fixed agenda. Both served his music well. As to the future relationship between Handel's new scores and his casts, Handel must have forseen that – as was normal – various amendments would be made between composition and performance, and between first performances and subsequent revivals, in order to suit the circumstances of particular casts of singers. While it is impossible to know for certain whether Handel was specifically imagining *Messiah* for four, five, six, or more soloists when he drafted his score, there are good reasons for regarding his initial autograph as a kind of abstract for the work as it would eventually come to performance.

When Jennens came up to London for his normal winter season at the end of November 1741, he was surprised to discover that Handel was not there, lending further weight to the supposition that the arrangements for Handel's Dublin season were made rather hurriedly. Clearly, also, there had been no communication between composer and librettist during the composition period of *Messiah*:

[CJ to EH]   Q.Square. Dec.2.1741

I heard with great pleasure at my arrival in Town, that Handel had set the Oratorio of Messiah; but it was some mortification to me to hear that instead of performing it here he was gone into Ireland with it. However, I hope we shall hear it when he comes back.

Any amendments to the libretto during composition must therefore have been made by Handel without referring back to Jennens. It is ironic, in view of Jennens's 'mortification', to find that the composer was following a career strategy that had been suggested by Holdsworth four and a half years previously:

[EH to CJ]   Winton. Mar. 15 1736/7

He wou'd do very well I think to ly quiet for a year or two, and then I am
persuaded y^t his [professional] enemies will sink of course, and many of them will
court him as much as now they oppose him.

The Dublin performances

Once in Dublin, Handel set up a subscription series of six performances.
His venue was not a theatre but a new concert room, the Great Music Hall
in Fishamble Street. This had been completed in 1741 for Dublin's
Charitable Musical Society, whose treasurer was William Neal, and it was
sometimes referred to as 'Mr Neal's Great Room'.[20] Between 23
December 1741 and 10 February 1742, Handel gave two performances
each of *L'Allegro*, *Acis and Galatea* and *Esther*. Jennens obviously expected
Handel to perform *Messiah* at some time during his stay in Dublin, because
almost directly he heard of Handel's absence from London he must have
forwarded to Handel the quotations from Virgil and the New Testament
for inclusion on the title page of the printed libretto. Handel wrote to
Jennens acknowledging the receipt of these, and recording the success of
his first subscription performance, *L'Allegro*:

[GFH to CJ]   Dublin Decem^{br} 29. 1741

it was with the greatest Pleasure I saw the Continuation of Your Kindness by the
Lines You was pleased to send me, in Order to be prefix'd to Your Oratorio
Messiah, which I set to Musick before I left England. I am emboldned, Sir, by the
generous Concern You please to take in relation to my affairs, to give You an
Account of the Success I have met here. The Nobility did me the Honour to make
amongst themselves a Subscription for 6 Nights, which did fill a Room of 600
Persons, so that I needed not sell one single Ticket at the Door, and without Vanity
the Performance was received with a general Approbation. Sig.^{ra} Avolio, which I
brought with me from London pleases extraordinary, I have form'd an other Tenor
Voice which gives great Satisfaction, the Basses and Counter Tenors are very good,
and the rest of the chorus Singers (by my Direction) do exceeding well, as for the
Instruments they are really excellent, Mr Dubourgh being at the Head of them, and
the Musick sounds delightfully in this charming Room, which puts me in such
Spirits (and my Health being so good) that I exert my self on my Organ with more
than usual Success. I opened with the Allegro, Penseroso, & Moderato, and I assure
you that the Words of the Moderato are vastly admired. The Audience being
composed (besides the Flower of Ladyes of Distinction and other People of the
greatest Quality) of so many Bishops, Deans, Heads of the Colledge, the most
eminents People in the Law as the Chancellor, Auditor General, &tc. all which are

15

very much taken with the Poetry. So that I am desired to perform it again the next time. I cannot sufficiently express the kind treatment I receive here, but the Politeness of this generous Nation cannot be unknown to You, so I let You judge of the Satisfaction I enjoy, passing my time with Honnour, profit, and pleasure. They propose already to have some more Performances, when the 6 Nights of the Subscription are over, and My Lord Duc the Lord Lieutenant (who is allways present with all His Family on those Nights) will easily obtain a longer Permission for me by His Majesty, so that I shall be obliged to make my stay here longer than I thought.

There is no mention here of Mrs. Cibber, who probably did not have a part in *L'Allegro* at Dublin. The tenor 'form'd' by Handel was probably James Bayleys (Bailey), a member of the choirs of Christ Church and St Patrick's Cathedrals.[21] Many of Handel's chorus singers and male soloists were probably also drawn from the same choirs, rather as his London oratorio chorus drew on singers from the ecclesiastical choirs.[22] However, Dean Swift at St Patrick's expressed strong disapproval of his Vicars Choral assisting 'at a club of fiddlers', and it is possible that the Cathedral singers had to withdraw after the fourth performance, leaving Handel with smaller forces.[23] Handel did not put Jennens's prefatory 'Lines' to *Messiah* into print for a few months, but coincidentally Jennens referred to his enthusiasm for introductory mottoes in a letter to Holdsworth:

[CJ to EH]   Q.Square. Feb 4. 1741-2

And as for Motto's in General, I find that many of our best Authors make use of them. For my own part, I own my self so much a Friend to them, that whenever I scribble to the publick, I cannot resist the Temptation of adorning my Title page with any significant motto that comes into my head & seems a propos: nay, I gave Handel a couple before an Oratorio [*Saul*], one Greek & the other Latin; not to show my acquaintance with the two Languages, but to point out more strongly my own Sentiments express'd in some parts of the Oratorio, & to justify them by two considerable Authoritys from the Heathen moralists.

In bringing together Virgil and St Paul on the cover of the *Messiah* word-book, Jennens was once again linking the authority of the 'heathen moralists' to that of the Judaeo-Christian tradition.

Before Handel's first subscription series in Dublin finished, he had already advertised a second series of six concerts. Each subscriber was entitled to three tickets for every performance, and Handel's advertisement suggests that the comfortable capacity of the hall was rather less than the '600 persons' referred to in his letter to Jennens:

No more than 150 Subscriptions will be taken in, and no Single Tickets sold or any Money taken at the Door. [*The Dublin Journal*, 6 February 1742][24]

Handel's second subscription consisted of two performances of *Alexander's Feast*, one revival each of *L'Allegro* and *Esther*, and two performances of the opera *Imeneo* as a 'Serenata' – an unstaged concert performance, and Handel's last public performances of an Italian work. The second subscription was a little more protracted, probably on account of the illness of Mrs Cibber, who had been given a part in *Alexander's Feast* and who was essential for *Imeneo*.

When the second subscription finished on 7 April 1742 it was probably too late in the year to embark on a third, but arrangements were already under way for another performance: Handel, presumably in collaboration with the Charitable Musical Society, had planned the first performance of *Messiah*:[25]

For Relief of the Prisoners in the several Gaols, and for the Support of Mercer's Hospital in Stephen's-street, and of the Charitable Infirmary on the Inns Quay, on Monday the 12th of April, will be performed at the Musick Hall in Fishamble Street, Mr. Handel's new Grand Oratorio call'd the Messiah, in which the Gentlemen of the Choirs of both Cathedrals will assist, with some Concertoes on the Organ, by Mr. Handell. Tickets to be had at the Musick Hall, and at Mr. Neal's in Christ-Church-Yard, at half a Guinea each.
N.B. No Person will be admitted to the Rehearsal without a Rehearsal Ticket, which will be given gratis with the Ticket for the Performance when pay'd for.
[*The Dublin Journal*, 23–27 March 1742]

The pre-history of the performance goes back even further: early in March a committee planning the charity performance had begun considering approaches to the Deans and Chapters of the Cathedrals to ask for the official corporate participation of the Cathedral choirs, and permission was apparently granted this time, in view of the charitable object of the performance.[26]

The newspaper reports concerning the Dublin première of *Messiah* are quite well known but demand extensive quotation because, even allowing for journalistic enthusiasm, they give a good impression of the positive spirit with which the performance was received. The performance was a 'Charity matinée', taking place at midday instead of at 7 p.m., the starting time of Handel's subscription performances.

Yesterday Morning, at the Musick Hall ... there was a public Rehearsal of the Messiah, Mr. Handel's new sacred Oratorio, which in the opinion of the best Judges, far surpasses anything of that Nature, which has been performed in this or any other Kingdom. The elegant Entertainment was conducted in the most regular Manner, and to the entire satisfaction of the most crowded and polite Assembly.

To the benefit of three very important public Charities, there will be a grand Performance of this Oratorio on Tuesday [13 April] next in the forenoon.
[*The Dublin News Letter*, 10 April 1742]

Yesterday Mr. Handell's new Grand Sacred Oratorio, called, The Messiah, was rehearsed ... to a most Grand, Polite and crouded Audience; and was performed so well, that it gave universal Satisfaction to all present; and was allowed by the greatest Judges to be the finest Composition of Musick that ever was heard, and the sacred Words as properly adapted for the Occasion.
N.B. At the Desire of several Persons of Distinction, the above Performance is put off to Tuesday next. The Doors will be opened at Eleven, and the Performance begin at Twelve.
Many Ladies and Gentlemen who are well-wishers to this Noble and Grand Charity for which this Oratorio was composed, request it as a Favour, that the Ladies who honour this Performance with their Presence would be pleased to come without Hoops [hoop-framed skirts], as it will greatly encrease the Charity, by making Room for more company.   [*The Dublin Journal*, 10 April 1742]

A similar advertisement on the day of the performance added, 'The Gentlemen are desired to come without their Swords', to increase audience accommodation yet further.[27]

On Tuesday last [13 April] Mr. Handel's Sacred Grand Oratorio, The Messiah, was performed at the New Musick-Hall in Fishamble-street, the best Judges allowed it to be the most finished piece of Musick. Words are wanting to express the exquisite Delight it afforded to the admiring crouded Audience. The Sublime, the Grand, and the Tender, adapted to the most elevated, majestick and moving Words, conspired to transport and charm the ravished Heart and Ear. It is but Justice to Mr. Handel, that the World should know, he generously gave the Money arising from this Grand Performance, to be equally shared by the Society for relieving Prisoners, the Charitable Infirmary, and Mercer's Hospital, for which they will ever gratefully remember his Name; and that the Gentlemen of the two Choirs, Mr. Dubourg, Mrs. Avolio, and Mrs. Cibber, who all performed their Parts to Admiration, acted also on the same disinterested Principle, satisfied with the deserved Applause of the Publick, and the conscious Pleasure of promoting such useful, and extensive Charity. There were about 700 People in the Room, and the Sum collected for that Noble and Pious Charity amounted to about 400 l. out of which 127 l. goes to each of the three great and pious Charities.   [*The Dublin Journal*, 13–17 April 1742]

The *Messiah* performance may have renewed Handel's popularity in Dublin. He had apparently decided in any case that there was an audience for a couple more performances. These were not advertised as charity performances, though tickets were sold from the houses of both Neal and Handel.[28] *Saul*, an ambitious score requiring more considerable forces than the works from Handel's subscription series, was (so the advertisement claimed) performed in response to the desire of 'several of the Nobility and Gentry' on 25 May, and there followed a second performance of *Messiah*, recorded by a single newspaper advertisement:

At the particular Desire of several of the Nobility and Gentry, on Thursday next, being the 3d Day of June, at the New Musick-Hall ... will be performed, Mr. Handel's new grand sacred Oratorio, called Messiah, with Concertos on the Organ. Tickets will be delivered at Mr. Handel's House in Abby-street, and at Mr. Neal's in Christ-church-yard, at half a Guinea each. A Rehearsal Ticket will be given gratis with the Ticket for the Performance. The Rehearsal will be on Tuesday the 1st of June at 12, and the Performance at 7 in the Evening. In order to keep the Room as cool as possible, a Pane of Glass will be removed from the Top of each of the Windows. – N.B. This will be the last Performance of Mr. Handel's during his Stay in this Kingdom.   [*The Dublin Journal*, 29 May–1 June 1742]

In addition to the soloists named in the newspaper report of 17 April (Avolio and Cibber), Handel's leading performers included a number of gentlemen from the Cathedral choirs who, while they did not perhaps have the stamina of Handel's London soloists, were nevertheless competent musicians. Handel accordingly shared the honours around. Names that Handel added to his conducting score show that the bass solos were divided between John Hill and John Mason, Bailey took the tenor part, and the alto role was divided between the contralto Mrs Cibber and the Cathedral altos William Lamb and Joseph Ward. For his male altos Handel even composed a new movement, the duet-and-chorus setting of 'How beautiful are the Feet' (36a/[38]/34b).

In view of *Messiah*'s subsequent reception in London, it is noteworthy that no word of criticism is known concerning the propriety of the work or the place of its performance in Dublin.[29] After the first performance, *The Dublin Journal* published a panegyric verse 'On Mr. Handel's Performance of his Oratorio, call'd the Messiah, for the Support of the Hospitals, and other pious Uses ... By Mr. L. White,' which included these lines:[30]

> To all the nobler Passions we are mov'd,
> When various strains repeated and improv'd,
> Express each different Circumstance and State,
> As if each Sound became articulate.

None but the Great Messiah cou'd inflame,
And raise his Soul to so sublime a Theme,
Profound the Thoughts, the Subject all divine.

The acceptance of *Messiah* is demonstrated yet more clearly by the memorandum written by Dr Edward Synge, Bishop of Elphin, after hearing one of Handel's performances of the oratorio:[31]

As Mr. Handel in his oratorio's greatly excells all other Composers I am acquainted with, So in the famous one, called The Messiah he seems to have excell'd himself. The whole is beyond any thing I had a notion of till I Read and heard it. It Seems to be a Species of Musick different from any other, and this is particularly remarkable of it. That tho' the Composition is very Masterly & artificial, yet the Harmony is So great and open, as to please all who have Ears & will hear, learned & unlearn'd. Without doubt this Superior Excellence is owing in some measure to the great care & exactness which Mr Handel seems to have us'd in preparing this Piece. But Some reasons may be given why He has Succeeded better in this than perhaps He could with all his skill, fully exerted, have done in any other.

1 one is the Subject, which is the greatest & most interesting. It Seems to have inspir'd him.
2 Another is the Words, which are all Sublime, or affecting in the greatest degree.
3 a Third reason for the Superior Excellence of this piece, 'Tis this there is no Dialogue. In every Drame there must be a great deal & often broken into very Short Speeches & Answers, If these be flat, & insipid, they move laughter or Contempt.

Whereas in this Piece the attention of the Audience is Engag'd from one end to the other: And the Parts Set in Recitativo, being Continu'd Sentences, & Some times adorn'd with to[o] much applause, by the audience as the rest. –

They Seem'd indeed throughly engag'd frome one end to the other. And, to their great honour, tho' the young & gay of both Sexes were present in great numbers, their behaviour was uniformly grave & decent, which Show'd that they were not only pleas'd but affected with the performance. Many, I hope, were instructed by it, and had proper Sentiments inspir'd in a Stronger Manner on their Minds.

Synge prefaced this remarkable piece of musical criticism to a plan for an oratorio, 'The Penitent', that he offered to Handel: he was clearly not in the least offended by any aspect of *Messiah*.

Handel's life and career naturally attracted anecdotes during the thirty years following his death, as the surviving people who had known the composer personally grew fewer while his music increased its hold on British musical life. Some of the anecdotes inevitably concerned *Messiah*, which had become his most popular work. Handel's early biographers,

Mainwaring and Burney, showed a remarkable ignorance of the historical record by stating that Handel performed *Messiah* in London before he went to Dublin.[32] Burney claimed that, while he was a schoolboy in Chester, he had seen Handel when he stopped there for some days on his journey to Ireland in 1741. This seems to lend plausibility to Burney's anecdote about Handel holding a trial rehearsal for sections of *Messiah* in Chester with a singer who could sing 'at sight' but not 'at first sight'. However, the authenticity of this anecdote is questionable;[33] it seems unlikely, in view of Handel's tight timetable between the completion of *Samson* and his arrival in Dublin, that he would be carrying performing material for *Messiah* with him, particularly as the new oratorio was not likely to be among his first productions in Ireland. Although the conducting score of *Messiah* was probably copied in London before Handel left, it is unlikely that the performer's part-books were entrusted to copyists until the performance was in sight. One or two of Handel's regular London copyists must have worked for him in Dublin, and in the autumn of 1741 they had much more urgent things to attend to in readiness for the first subscription series there.[34]

One anecdote concerning the Dublin performances of *Messiah* runs as follows:

Mrs. Cibber, in *The Messiah*, in Dublin, executed her airs so pathetically, that Dr. Delany, the great friend and companion of Swift, exclaimed, as he sat in the boxes, 'Woman, for this, be all thy sins forgiven'.[35]

Since Mrs Cibber performed *Messiah* in Dublin only in 1742, the story, if true, must relate to Handel's own performances. Its origin is obscure, but it is not implausible. Patrick Delany was in Dublin during this period, and the anecdote preserves an artistic, if not a factual, truth relating to Mrs Cibber's histrionic strength in 'pathetic' airs.[36] According to Sheridan:

it was not to any extraordinary powers of voice (whereof she had but a moderate share) nor to a greater degree of skill in musick (wherein many of the Italians must be allowed to exceed her) that she owed her excellence, but to expression only.[37]

Burney, probably elaborating from Sheridan's description, concluded that:

by a natural pathos, and perfect conception of the words, she often penetrated the heart, when others, with infinitely greater skill, could only reach the ear.[38]

The music and soloists in Handel's Dublin performances

It is difficult to establish precisely the chronology of some of Handel's earliest revisions to his score of *Messiah*, but before the first performance he certainly recomposed the opening of 'Thus saith the Lord' (producing version 4/5/5) and the end of 'Why do the nations' (from 38a/40i/36 to 38/40ii/36x), and probably shortened 'Rejoice greatly' (from –/A7/16a to 16a/17ii/16ax), 'O death, where is thy sting' (from –/A15/44 to 48/50/44x) and reduced 'The trumpet shall sound' from a *Da Capo* to a *Dal Segno* reprise aria. These revised versions became standard for Handel's subsequent performances, and it is very doubtful whether Handel ever performed the versions from his original autograph. Two further amendments were made for Dublin. The sequence 'Then shall the eyes – He shall feed his flock – Come unto him', composed originally for soprano, was transposed down for Mrs Cibber, who also received 'If God be for us'. In the latter case, more than simple transposition was involved: Handel recomposed details of the cadence-points in the violin parts for the alto version (50a/52ii/–). This alto version was also retained in Handel's first London performances of *Messiah*.[39] 'But who may abide' may have been sung as a recitative in Dublin, though the authenticity of the recitative setting that appears in two later *Messiah* sources is not beyond question.[40]

One mystery concerning Handel's cast in Dublin must be mentioned. Apart from the conducting score and newspaper reports, the principal source of information is a copy of the word-book for the Dublin performances annotated with singers' names.[41] These generally agree with those in the conducting score, but the word-book does not mention Avolio: instead the soprano solos are designated for 'McLean', presumably the wife of 'Mr Maclaine' the organist, who was reported as arriving in Dublin to perform for Handel in November 1741. Nothing else is known of Mrs McLean as a member of Handel's cast, and the newspaper report of the first *Messiah* performance specifically refers to Avolio. Unless Signora Avolio and Mrs McLean were the same person, or the annotated word-book is in some way misleading, an explanation of the discrepancy might be that McLean took over Avolio's part for the second performance. Avolio was still in Dublin at the same time, however: she gave a farewell benefit concert on 23 June.[42]

3

The first London performances

On 13 August 1742 Handel left Dublin,[1] and he was back in London by
early September:

[EH to CJ]   London 7ber [September] 10 1742

I suppose you have heard of Mr Handel's return to London, wh^{ch} wou'd have been a
great joy to you, if you did not at ye same time hear that He is to return again to
Ireland for ye winter.

By then, a letter from Handel himself was on its way to Jennens, outlining
his future plans and enclosing the Bishop of Elphin's comments on *Messiah*
that were quoted in chapter 2:

[GFH to CJ]   London Septr 9.th 1742

It was indeed Your humble Servant which intended You a visit in my way from
Ireland to London, for I certainly could have given You a better account by word of
mouth, as by writing, how well Your Messiah was received in that Country, yet as a
Noble Lord, and no less than the Bishop of Elphin (a Nobleman very learned in
Musick) has given his Observation in writing of this Oratorio, I send you here
annexed the Contents of it in his own words. – I shall send the printed Book of the
Messiah to Mr Isted for You. As for my Success in General in that generous and polite
Nation, I reserve the account of it till I have the Honour to see you in London. The
report that the Direction of the Opera next winter is comitted to my Care, is
groundless. The gentlemen who have undertaken to middle with Harmony can not
agree, and are quite in a Confusion. Whether I shall do some thing in the Oratorio way
(as several of my friends desire) I can not determine as yet. Certain it is that this time
12 month I shall continue my Oratorio's in Ireland, where they are going to make a
large Subscription allready for that Purpose . . . I think it a very long time to the month
of November next when I can have some hopes of seeing You here in Town.

On the basis of this Jennens was able to write to Holdsworth:

[CJ to EH]   Gops. Oct.29. 1742

You was misinformed about Mr Handel, who does not return to Ireland till next

Winter, so that I hope to have some very agreeable Entertainments from him this Season. His Messiah by all accounts is his Masterpiece.

Handel gave notice of his forthcoming London entertainments – 'some thing in the oratorio way' – by sending the libretto of *Samson* (whose score he had completed and extensively revised in October 1742) to the Inspector of Stage Plays in January 1743,[2] and then advertising a subscription series of six performances at Covent Garden (on much the same basis as his Dublin subscriptions) in the London newspapers for 12 February.

Meanwhile, Handel's relationship with Jennens had turned sour and the tone of Jennens's references to *Messiah* changed abruptly:

[CJ to EH]   Q. Square. Jan. 17. 1742–3

He [Handel] has compos'd an exceeding fine Oratorio, being an alteration of Milton's Samson Agonistes, with which he is to begin Lent. His Messiah has disappointed me, being set in great hast, tho' he said he would be a year about it, & make it the best of all his Compositions. I shall put no more Sacred Words into his hands, to be thus abus'd.

Presumably Jennens did not know that *Samson* had been drafted in nearly as much 'hast' as *Messiah*. At that stage Jennens may have examined carefully the copy of the Dublin word-book for *Messiah* that Handel had sent him, but he had heard no performance and it is doubtful whether he had seen a score.[3] His feelings received a sympathetic response at the end of Holdsworth's next letter:

[EH to CJ]   16 Febr. 1743

I am sorry to hear yr. friend Handel is such a jew. His negligence, to say no worse, has been a great disappointment to others as well as y^r self, for I hear there was great expectation of his composition. I hope the words, tho' murther'd, are still to be seen, and yt I shall have that pleasure when I return. And as I don't understand the musick I shall be better off than the rest of ye world.

Unfortunately, this may have fuelled Jennens's annoyance with Handel further. When he wrote back to Holdsworth after Handel's first subscription performance, he even seemed to hold it against the composer that the subscription had begun with *Samson* rather than *Messiah*:

[CJ to EH]   Q. Square Feb. 21 1742–3

As to the Messiah, 'tis still in his power by retouching the weak parts to make it fit for a publick performance; & I have said a great deal to him on the Subject; but he is so lazy & so obstinate, that I much doubt the Effect. I have a copy, as it was printed in Ireland, full of Bulls; & if he does not print a correct one here, I shall do it my Self, & perhaps tell him a piece of my mind by way of Preface. I am a little out of humour, as you may perceive, & want to vent my Spleen for ease. What adds to my chagrin is, that if he makes his Oratorio ever so perfect, there is a clamour about Town, said to arise from the B^{ps}, against performing it. This may occasion some enlargement of the Preface.

[Post-script:] Last Friday Handel perform'd his Samson, a most exquisite Entertainment, which tho' I heard with infinite Pleasure, yet it increas'd my resentment for his neglect of the Messiah. You do him too much Honour to call him a Jew! a Jew would have paid more respect to the Prophets. The Name of Heathen will suit him better. Yet a sensible Heathen would not have prefer'd the Nonsense, foisted by one Hamilton into Milton's Samson Agonistes, to the sublime Sentiments & expressions of Isaiah & David, of the Apostles & Evangelists, & of Jesus Christ.

Handel put on six performances of *Samson* to good houses,[4] and advanced to a second subscription series which began on 16 March with yet another performance of *Samson*, followed by *L'Allegro* two days later, and then, at last, *Messiah* on Wednesday 23 March. On 19 March two newspapers, *The Daily Advertiser* and *The London Daily Post*, carried notices for the performance, advertised under the title 'A New Sacred Oratorio', but *The Universal Spectator*, published on the same day, carried a lengthy article giving some substance to Jennens's chance remark a month before about the 'clamour about Town, said to arise from the B^{ps} [? Bishops] against performing it [*Messiah*]':[5]

The following Letter may to many of my Readers, especially those of a gay and polite Taste, seem too rigid a Censure on a Performance, which is so universally approv'd: However, I could not suppress it, as there is so well-intended a Design and pious Zeal runs through the whole, and nothing derogatory said of Mr. *Handel's* Merit. Of what good Consequences it will produce, I can only say – *Valeat Quantum valere potest.*

To the AUTHOR of the UNIVERSAL SPECTATOR.

Sir,

My ... Purpose ... is to consider, and, if possible, induce others to consider, the Impropriety of *Oratorios*, as they are now perform'd.

Before I speak against them (that I may not be thought to do it out of Prejudice or Party) it may not be improper to declare, that I am a profess'd Lover of *Musick*, and in particular all Mr. *Handel's Performances*, being *one* of the *few* who never deserted him. I am also a great Admirer of *Church Musick*, and think no other equal to it, nor any Person so capable to compose it, as Mr. *Handel*. To return: An *Oratorio* either is an *Act of Religion*, or it is not; if it is, I ask if the *Playhouse* is a fit *Temple* to perform it in, or a Company of *Players* fit *Ministers* of *God's Word*, for in that Case such they are made . . .

In the other Case, if it is not perform'd as an *Act* of *Religion*, but for *Diversion* and *Amusement* only (and indeed I believe few or none go to an *Oratorio* out of *Devotion*), what a *Prophanation* of *God*'s Name and Word is this, to make so light Use of them? . . . How must it offend a devout *Jew*, to hear the great *Jehovah*, the *proper* and most *sacred Name of God* (a Name a *Jew*, if not a *Priest*, hardly dare pronounce) sung, I won't say to a light Air (for as Mr. *Handel* compos'd it, I dare say it is not) but by a Set of People very *unfit* to *perform* so *solemn* a *Service*. *David* said, *How can we sing the Lord's Song in a strange Land*; but sure he would have thought it much stranger to have heard it sung in a *Playhouse*.

But it seems the *Old Testament* is not to be prophan'd alone, nor *God* by the *Name of Jehovah* only, but the *New* must be join'd with it, and *God* by the most *sacred* the most *merciful Name* of *Messiah*; for I'm inform'd that an Oratorio call'd by that Name has already been perform'd in *Ireland*, and is soon to be perform'd *here*: What the Piece itself is, I know not, and therefore shall say nothing about it; but I must again ask, If the *Place* and *Performers* are fit? As to the Pretence that there are many Persons who will say their *Prayers* there who will not go to *Church*, I believe I may venture to say, that the Assertion is *false*, without *Exception*; for I can never believe that Persons who have so little regard for Religion, as to think it not worth their while to go to *Church* for it, will have any *Devotion* on hearing a *religious* Performance in a *Playhouse*.

... PHILALETHES.
[*The Universal Spectator*, 19 March 1743]

The deference shown to Handel and his music by both 'Philalethes' and the editor of the newspaper is surely a reflection of the success of Handel's oratorio subscriptions: in contrast to the period before 1741, when the influential section of London's theatre-going public was perceived as being indifferent or opposed to Handel's music,[6] Handel was now a force to be reckoned with. 'Philalethes' does not attack Handel's music, or even the idea of *Messiah* as an oratorio, but questions the suitability of the subject for theatre performance; like Jennens, he was attacking the work before it had been performed in London.

With *Messiah*, the potential problems of public acceptance for theatre oratorio, and the inherent artistic tensions of the genre itself (relying as it did on the application of theatrical musical conventions to a sacred story), came to a head. The compartmentalisation between 'Sacred' and 'Secular' that characterised some religious thinking in Britain could not cope with the idea of 'A New Sacred Oratorio' in the theatre, a title that, ironically, may have inflamed opinion more than 'Messiah'. Theatres were regarded by many religious reformers as places of evil influence from which people had to be redeemed.[7] Handel had received a warning shot in 1732 when the Chapel Royal boys were prevented from taking part in staged performances at a public theatre. It is difficult to know whether the attitudes put forward by 'Philalethes' were very influential among London society, or among Handel's audiences: in spite of the writer's professed enthusiasm for Handel's performances, it is difficult to believe that someone who regarded the theatre as a venue for 'Light and vain, prophane and dissolute pieces' would go there very often. Many a contemporary theatre-goer or performer would have been as offended as Handel by the stance taken by 'Philalethes', and the argument needed only a little extension to call into question all of Handel's theatre oratorio performances.

The issue was not one of simple opposition between religious and theatrical interests in London; 'Philalethes's' letter was answered by a rejoinder in another newspaper that challenged the idea of excluding religion from the theatre:

Wrote extempore by a Gentleman, on reading the *Universal Spectator*.

On Mr. HANDEL's *new ORATORIO,*
perform'd at the Theatre Royal in Covent-Garden.

Cease, Zealots, cease to blame these Heav'nly Lays,
For Seraphs fit to sing Messiah's Praise!
Nor, for your trivial Argument, assign,
'The Theatre not fit for Praise Divine.'

These hallow'd Lays to Musick give new Grace,
To Virtue Awe, and sanctify the Place;
To Harmony, like his, Celestial Pow'r is giv'n,
T'exalt the Soul from Earth, and make, of Hell, a Heav'n.

[*The Daily Advertiser*, 31 March 1743]

This provoked a further reply from 'Philalethes', partially in verse but restating rather than advancing his side of the argument:

Mistake me not, I blam'd no heav'nly Lays;
Nor *Handel*'s Art which strives a Zeal to raise,
In every Soul to sing *Messiah*'s Praise:
But if to *Seraphs* you the Task assign;
Are *Players* fit for *Ministry Divine?*
Or *Theatres* for *Seraphs* there to sing,
The holy Praises of their Heav'nly King?

[*The Universal Spectator*, 16 April 1743]

Thirty-seven years later James Beattie put two tales about the first London performances of *Messiah* into a letter to Revd Dr Laing:

I lately heard two anecdotes, which deserve to be put in writing and which you will be glad to hear. When Handel's 'Messiah' was first performed, the audience was exceedingly struck and affected by the music in general; but when that chorus struck up, 'For the Lord God Omnipotent reigneth', they were so transported that they all, together with the king (who happened to be present), started up, and remained standing till the chorus ended: and hence it became the fashion in England for the audience to stand while that part of the music is performing. Some days after the first exhibition of the same divine oratorio, Mr. Handel came to pay his respect to lord Kinnoull, with whom he was particularly acquainted. His lordship, as was natural, paid him some compliments on the noble entertainment which he had lately given the town. 'My lord,' said Handel, 'I should be sorry if I only entertained them, I wish to make them better.' These two anecdotes I had from lord Kinnoull himself. You will agree with me, that the first does great honour to Handel, to music, and to the English nation: the second tends to confirm my theory, and sir John Hawkins testimony, that Handel, in spite of all that has been said to the contrary, must have been a pious man.[8]

Anything written so long after the event must be regarded with due caution. Handel's reported words seem rather out of character: he was temperamentally a dramatist rather than a preacher. On the other hand, it remains a common experience that composers and performers rarely give considered responses when interviewed about their work close to the event: allowance must be made not only for the proximity of the performance experience itself, but also for pressures Handel may have been under from religious zealots and also from his librettist, which would naturally make him defensive.

As to Beattie's explanation for the origins of the British custom of standing up for the 'Hallelujah' chorus, the fundamental question must be not whether King George II stood up at the first performance, but whether he was present at all. The last occasion on which the King is known to have attended one of Handel's theatre performances was the first performance of *Saul* in January 1739. It may be that royal attendances at Handel's oratorio subscriptions (unlike visits to the opera), were undertaken in a private capacity, and went unreported. It is remarkable, nevertheless, that neither newspapers nor contemporary diarists make any reference to the King's attendance at the later oratorios.[9] In view of the controversy that had preceded the first London performance of *Messiah*, the King would probably have been advised to stay away, especially if bishops had been among the objectors. On the other hand, in favour of Beattie's account, his source for the anecdotes, Lord Hay of Kinnoull, was in London during the period when *Messiah* was first performed.[10]

It is perhaps surprising that Beattie's letter contains no hint of the controversy surrounding *Messiah*'s first performance, and we might wonder whether a couple of newspaper articles and some references in Jennens's letters give a falsely inflated view of the controversy's effects. But one contemporary and associate of Handel's, the Earl of Shaftesbury, was quite clear on the matter in his own recollections:[11]

In Lent 1743, at Covent Garden he performed his Oratorio of Samson, and it was received with uncommon Applause. He afterwards performed The Messiah. But partly from the Scruples, some Persons had entertained, against carrying on such a Performance in a Play House, and partly for not entering into the genius of the Composition, this Capital Composition, was but indifferently relish'd.

Whatever the pressures from a section of London's religious community against *Messiah*, they did not prevent Handel from completing his second subscription successfully with three performances of *Messiah* and one of *Samson*, finishing on 31 March. Although the work appeared modestly in the advertisements as 'A New Sacred Oratorio', the word-book for the 1743 performances carried the title *Messiah*. After the first night, Jennens was a little more positive towards Handel's music:

[CJ to EH]   Q.Square. Mar.24. 1742–3

Messiah was perform'd last night, & will be again to morrow, notwithstanding the clamour rais'd against it, which has only occasion'd it's being advertis'd without its Name; a Farce, which gives me as much offence as any thing relating to the performance can give the B^s. & other squeamish People. 'Tis after all, in the main, a fine Composition, notwithstanding some weak parts, which he was too idle & too obstinate to retouch, tho' I us'd great importunity to perswade him to it. He & his Toad-eater Smith did all they could to murder the Words in print; but I hope I have restor'd them to Life, not without much difficulty.

Only a single copy of the 1743 word-book is known, and perhaps only a limited run was printed in view of the controversy surrounding the first performance.[12] Since the word-book was apparently produced under Jennens's watchful eye, it presents an authoritative text, and is probably fairly close to Jennens's original: its principal features are collated with the text of Handel's autographs in Appendix I. The word-book includes section divisions, equivalent to 'scenes' within the three Parts.

Handel's 1743 cast was described none too flatteringly by Horace Walpole after the second performance of *Samson*.[13]

Arlington Street, Feb.24, 1743

Handel has set up an Oratorio against the Operas, and succeeds. He has hired all the goddesses from farces and the singers of Roast Beef from between the acts at both theatres, with a man with one note in his voice, and a girl without ever an one; and so they sing, and make brave hallelujahs; and the good company encore the recitative, if it happens to have an cadence like what they call a tune.

Both *Samson* and *Messiah* had to be adapted to accommodate a large cast of eight soloists, but there were important differences between this cast and the large team that Handel had employed in Dublin. Handel had not previously worked with any of the singers in his Dublin company: apart from Avolio, he had had to form new relationships with all of them, and the situation was dominated by the type of soloists contributed by the Dublin cathedral choirs. In 1743, Handel's London company included singers who had worked with him before. From Dublin he retained Avolio, Cibber and Dubourg, the leader of the orchestra. The tenor John Beard, the basses William Savage and Thomas Reinhold, and the soprano Miss Edwards had sung for Handel in his previous London companies: all were intelligent and highly professional performers. The 'goddesses from the Farces' seems to refer to two actresses-turned-singers, Mrs Cibber and Mrs Clive. Mrs Clive, a new acquisition from the Drury Lane company, who was cast as Dalila in *Samson*, may well, like Mrs Cibber, have made her mark by presentation and characterisation rather than by natural musical gifts. The other singer new to Handel's company was the tenor Thomas Lowe, also previously from Drury Lane.[14] If Burney's description of the singers is to be trusted, Beard and Lowe formed an interesting contrast: Beard was intelligent, both in musical matters and in conveying dramatic characterisation, while Lowe, even though he possessed a strikingly good voice, was deficient in expression and musical versatility.[15]

The music of Handel's 1743 performances

Most of the score of *Messiah*, as it stood after the Dublin performances, could be adapted for the 1743 cast by a simple re-allocation of solo music.[16] Handel also composed new music for the first London performances. The aria setting of 'But lo, the angel of the Lord' (14a/A6/13a) was composed for Mrs Clive, to replace the accompanied recitative

(14/14(b)/13): Handel never used it after 1743, and it must be directly associated with this particular singer. The text 'Their sound is gone out into all Lands' had not figured in the Dublin performances, although it was certainly in the original libretto; in Handel's composition autograph it was set as the 'B' section of the *da capo* aria 'How beautiful are the Feet' (–/A13/34a, never performed in full). As already noted, Handel replaced this aria (which began with the text from Romans x,15) before the first Dublin performance with the duet-and-chorus movement to the similar text from Isaiah lii, 7,9 (36/[38]/34). Jennens apparently condoned the retention of the duet-and-chorus (now sung by Avolio and Cibber, 36ax/[38x]/–), but presumably insisted that the text 'Their sound is gone out into all Lands' be restored, and Handel composed another short aria (37a/39ii/35) to accommodate this. He also composed a new setting of 'Thou art gone up on high' for one of the sopranos (34b/A10/32b),[17] and adapted his original bass aria setting of 'But who may abide' for the tenor Lowe. Handel's early performing versions of 'But who may abide' constitute one of the few areas of his score that cannot be retrieved entirely from surviving sources. The Dublin word-book designated the movement a 'Recitative', which might be the movement found in some much later sources (5a/A5/0),[18] on the other hand, the word-book may have been in error here, and the bass aria from Handel's autograph (5b/A2/6a) may have been performed. Handel adapted this for Lowe in 1743: a shortened form (5bx/–/–) is recoverable,[19] but any other alterations arising from the change of voice are lost.

One other feature of the 1743 *Messiah* performances is of importance. It appears that, either shortly before the first London performance of *Messiah* or (perhaps more likely) between performances, Beard became indisposed or left Handel's company.[20] Having carefully allocated his music in the first place, Handel obviously adjusted to the new situation in a way that would cause least confusion. His solution was to transfer Beard's music almost completely to Avolio, a tribute to her musicianship and perhaps a negative reflection on Lowe.[21] The unique allocation of 'Ev'ry valley', 'All they that see Him' and 'He that dwelleth/Thou shalt break them' to the soprano was clearly a temporary response to a practical emergency.

4

Revival and revision, 1743–1759

Although Handel successfully completed his second subscription series in March 1743, the season took its toll on his health. To the tensions caused by the 'clamour' over the performances of *Messiah* were added disagreements with two of his most essential friends, his copyist–manager John Christopher Smith and Jennens himself.[1] *The Daily Advertiser* for 11 April 1743 reported: 'Mr. Handel, who has been dangerously ill, is now recover'd', but Jennens remained concerned:

[CJ to EH]   Gops. Apr. 29 1743

I hear Handel has a return of his Paralytick Disorder, which affects his Head & Speech. He talks of spending a year abroad, so that we are to expect no Musick next year; & since the Town has lost it's only Charm, I'll stay in the Country as long as ever I can.

Shortly after, on May 4, Horace Walpole wrote: 'We are likely at last to have no Opera next year: Handel has had a palsy, and can't compose'.[2] In fact, Handel recovered sufficiently quickly to compose *Semele* and the *Dettingen Te Deum* during June and July. He then turned his mind towards a new oratorio for his next season and, avoiding Jennens, went to James Miller for *Joseph and his Brethren*, composed during August and September. By then plans for a return to Dublin, or for a convalescent year abroad, must have been set aside.

Unfortunately the recovery of Handel's health rendered him vulnerable to renewed pressure over *Messiah* from Jennens:

[CJ to EH]   Gops. Sept. 15. 1743

I hear Handel is perfectly recover'd, & has compos'd a new Te Deum & a new Anthem against the return of his Master from Germany. I don't yet despair of making him retouch the Messiah, at least he shall suffer for his negligence; nay I am inform'd that he has suffer'd, for he told Ld Guernsey, that a letter I wrote him about it contributed to the bringing of his last illness upon him; & it is reported that being a little delirious with a Fever, he said he should be damn'd for preferring

Dagon (a Gentleman he was very complaisant to in the Oratorio of Samson) before the Messiah. This shews that I gall'd him: but I have not done with him yet.

Holdsworth urged Jennens to be more conciliatory and suggested that Gopsal was having a bad effect on Jennens's temper:

[EH to CJ]   Florence. Oct. 28. 1743

It has had an ill effect upon you, and made you quarrel with your best friends, Virgil & Handel. You have contributed, by y.ʳ own confession, to give poor Handel a fever, and now He is pretty well recover'd, you seem resolv'd to attack him again; for you say you have not yet done with him. This is really ungenerous, & not like Mr. Jennens. Pray be merciful; and don't you turn Samson, & use him like a Philistine.

But Jennens was in no mood to accept either point:

[CJ to EH]   Gops. Dec.5. 1743

It is not Leic[ester]shire that has made me quarrel with Handel, but his own Folly, (to say no worse), if that can be called a quarrel, where I only tell him the Truth; & he knows it to be Truth, yet is so obstinate, he will not submit to it.

Notwithstanding opposition from the disgruntled patrons of the opera company, Handel successfully ran a subscription season of twelve performances during February and March 1744, with the new works *Semele* and *Joseph*, and revivals of *Samson* and *Saul*. Mrs Delany expected *Messiah* to be performed as well and, since she was a personal acquaintance of the composer, her expectation may have been realistically based on a plan of Handel's.[3] Perhaps Handel thought better of it, lest an immediate revival should rekindle controversy; a revival would also entail confrontation with Jennens. It is of some significance that Mrs Delany expected *Messiah* to be Handel's last performance of the season, which fell on the Wednesday before Easter. When Handel came to revive *Messiah*, it was always as his last performance of the theatre season, and usually within the fortnight before Easter – a fact worth noting today, when *Messiah* is more often performed at Christmas.

One unfortunate event was the death of the librettist of *Joseph* on 26 April 1744 which drove Handel back to Jennens:

[CJ to EH]   Q. Square. May 7. 1744

Handel has promis'd to revise the Oratorio of Messiah, & He & I are very good Friends again. The reason is he has lately lost his Poet Miller, & wants to set me at work for him again.

On 9 June Handel wrote to Jennens (now at Gopsal) outlining his plans for the next season.[4] Jennens agreed to provide Handel with a new oratorio libretto (*Belshazzar*), and Handel took the initiative about *Messiah*. On 19 July 1744 he wrote: 'Be pleased to point out those passages in the Messiah which You think require altering.'

The 1745 revival

Handel set himself a very ambitious programme of twenty-four subscription performances in the Haymarket theatre, beginning with Saturday presentations but ending with Wednesday and Friday performances during Lent. *Deborah* (3 November 1744) came too early for the patrons, 'as the greatest part of Mr. Handel's subscribers are not in Town'. Two performances each of *Semele* and *Hercules* followed during December and January. After this Handel seems to have realised that, even in the absence of competition from the opera company, he had over-reached himself. After six performances, he offered to refund subscribers three quarters of their money.[5] According to Jennens, 'Most of them refus'd to take back their Money, upon which he resolv'd to begin again in Lent.'[6] Handel did indeed begin on the first Friday of Lent (1745), and presented ten performances including *Samson, Saul, Joseph, Belshazzar* and, on the Tuesday and Thursday of Holy Week, *Messiah*.[7]

The 1745 revival of *Messiah* seems to have passed without controversy; the audience's main attention was probably focused on the new oratorio *Belshazzar*. *Messiah* was this time advertised under its own name. No word-book for this revival survives, nor for the 1745 performances of *Samson, Saul* or *Joseph*: perhaps only the new oratorio was printed afresh and the others were sold from previous stock. Handel's 1745 performances of *Messiah* are among the most difficult to reconstruct precisely. The cast included the soprano 'La Francesina' (Elisabeth Duparc), the mezzo-soprano Miss Robinson (who only sang for Handel during the 1744–5 season) and the stalwarts John Beard and Thomas Reinhold. Handel's various revisions to the singers' names in the conducting score of *Messiah* include many entries attributable to 1745.[8]

However, the 1745 revival of *Messiah* is of the greatest interest because it must have included some revisions undertaken at Jennens's insistence. Two new settings were certainly composed for the revival.[9] We may surmise that Jennens found Handel's 1743 aria, 'Their sound is gone out', too bland for its purpose: something stronger was needed to provoke a reaction in the following movement, 'Why do the nations?' Accordingly, Handel composed a chorus (37/39/35a), and restored the 'A' section of his original aria version of 'How beautiful are the Feet' (36/38i/34ax) to precede it.[10] Handel's other new setting, the re-casting of 'Rejoice greatly' into common time, was probably undertaken to reduce the excessive amount of compound metre at the end of Part One.[11]

Messiah is mentioned in one further letter from Jennens, dated 30 August 1745:

In your last letter but one you talk'd something of reading a foolish hasty performance of mine [?*Belshazzar*], but 'tis not fit for your perusal; therefore think no more of it: but I shall show you a collection I gave Handel, call'd Messiah, which I value highly, & he has made a fine Entertainment of it, tho' not near so good as he might & ought to have done. I have with great difficulty made him correct some of the grossest faults in the composition, but he retain'd his Overture obstinately, in which there are some passages far unworthy of Handel, but much more unworthy of the Messiah.[12]

The concentration of Jennens's criticism on the overture seems odd, but it may have been the only movement of *Messiah* for which he had the music. If he had not yet received his manuscript copy of the score,[13] his knowledge of *Messiah*'s music would have been confined to published material. The overture to *Messiah* (entitled 'The Sacred Oratorio') was included in the eighth collection of Handel's overtures published by Walsh in 1743: orchestral part-books appeared in July of that year, and a two-stave arrangement 'for the Improvement of the Hand on the Harpsicord or Spinnet' in December.[14] The only other movement to appear in print at this early stage was 'He was despised', in a volume of *Sonatas or Chamber Aires, for a German Flute, Violin or Harpsichord*, obviously intended, like the keyboard version of the overture, for domestic performance.[15]

After 1745 Jennens fades from the picture of *Messiah*'s development. No doubt the traumatic experience of the advance and defeat of the Jacobite uprising in 1745–6 increased the discomfort and isolation of his social position. Jennens was even reluctant to come up to London to hear Handel's oratorios in January 1746,[16] and he provided no more libretti for him. The crisis in London's public life aborted Handel's 1746 oratorio season after only three performances of the *Occasional Oratorio*. In that year he returned to Covent Garden theatre as his permanent venue. In subsequent seasons he abandoned the subscription system, giving independent theatre performances in seasons based around the Lenten period of March–April. During 1747–8, his new oratorios were based on Old Testament subjects that clearly had a topical relevance, treating victorious heroes such as Judas Maccabaeus and Joshua; *Messiah* was not revived until 1749.

1749–1753: Covent Garden and the Foundling Hospital

In musical content, Handel's single performance on Maundy Thursday 1749 seems to have been fundamentally the same as his 1745 performances, though the cast was different. Beard was out of Handel's company during 1749 and 1750, and Lowe took his place. Two singers who were to serve *Messiah* well appeared for the first time, the soprano Giulia Frasi and the contralto Caterina Galli. Only Reinhold retained his place from the 1745 cast. In addition to Frasi, Handel had a boy treble soloist, and he divided the upper-voice music diplomatically.[17] 'If God is for us' was performed in the original version for soprano voice, probably for the first time. Although Lowe retained most of the tenor role, the sequence of four movements beginning 'Thy Rebuke hath broken his Heart' (composed originally for tenor, and probably divided between Avolio and Lowe in 1743) was allocated to the upper voices: it may have been divided between Frasi and the treble, though it is more likely that Frasi sang all four movements. In subsequent years Handel subjected this sequence to a variety of treatments: all-soprano, all-tenor, soprano/treble and soprano/tenor.[18] In addition to the relevant markings on Handel's conducting score, an important source of evidence for his performances of 1749, 1752 and 1753 is a copy of the printed word-book for 1749, marked up in manuscript with the names of soloists.[19]

Perhaps the most interesting feature of Handel's 1749 version is his orchestral 'ripieno' directions. He only added 'con ripieno' and 'senza ripieno' markings consistently throughout the scores of oratorios presented in 1749: the new *Susanna* and *Solomon*, and the revivals of *Samson*, *Hercules* and *Messiah*. Examination of all five scores reveals that these directions relate to the employment of an unusually large string section (his 'normal' section comprised about twenty-five players). The 'ripieno' directions define the participation of the additional string players: they are not instructions for occasional reduction to a small concertino group. There is no evidence that the large string group was matched by a correspondingly large wind ensemble, though woodwind parts may have been doubled as a matter of course. Although Handel's 'ripieno' directions may be of practical value in modern performances with an exceptionally large string group, their significance should not be over-emphasised: they applied to only one performance, and were added in response to a specifically luxurious situation.[20]

Another performance that Handel gave in 1749 held more long-term significance: on 27 May he gave a midday charity performance in the chapel of the Foundling Hospital. Thus began his association with the Hospital for the Maintenance and Education of Exposed and Deserted Young Children, a charity barely ten years old and in need of funds for its building and maintenance programme: the chapel itself was still unfinished, with no glass in the windows, when Handel gave his first concert there.[21] The concert, attended by the Prince and Princess of Wales, ended with Handel's 'Foundling Hospital Anthem', *Blessed are they that considereth the Poor and Needy*. The anthem was partly assembled from movements borrowed from earlier works, and for the last movement he used the 'Hallelujah' chorus: perhaps it was on this occasion that royalty first stood for the movement. (Since *Messiah* had only received a single performance since 1745, it is unlikely that a large proportion of the Hospital audience would have recognised its origin.) Also in 1749, two arias from *Messiah* were published for the first time, in the first volume of Walsh's anthology *Handel's Songs Selected from His Latest Oratorios*.[22] Like Walsh's edition of the overture, the *Songs* came in two versions: a two-stave keyboard score, and instrumental parts. The other arias appeared in Walsh's collections over the next ten years, so that eventually every *Messiah* aria was represented with one version in print.[23]

On Maundy Thursday 1750 Handel once more concluded his oratorio season at Covent Garden with *Messiah*. At this period he made his last significant compositional revisions to the score, inspired by a new member of his cast, the alto castrato Gaetano Guadagni. He had six soloists: Frasi and a boy for the upper parts, Galli and Guadagni in the alto register, Lowe and Reinhold as tenor and bass. Some re-allocation of music was called for, particularly to accommodate two alto-register soloists, and Handel composed two new settings for Guadagni of arias formerly allocated to bass and soprano (5/6i/6 and 34/36i/32). Like the performance of 1749, the 1750 Covent Garden revival seems to have passed without incident or controversy, though it is likely that Guadagni's presence attracted some attention to Handel's oratorio season as a whole. But another performance of *Messiah* three weeks later was to transform the work's reputation in London drastically.

During 1749–50 the Foundling Hospital chapel was nearing completion, and the Governors began to plan an official opening. Approaches were made to the Archbishop of Canterbury to preach, and to Handel for some music. However, early in March 1750 this plan was dropped: perhaps it was discovered that the building would not be finished in time, and in any case the Hospital had taken no steps towards appointing a Chaplain. Instead Handel was approached for a 'Performance of Musick and Voices', and the occasion was converted into an official 'opening' for the organ he had donated to the chapel. This time Handel decided to perform *Messiah*. The performance on 1 May attracted a huge audience: 1,500 tickets were prepared, and 1,386 were officially sold. The chapel was tightly packed and people still had to be turned away; at a repeat performance a fortnight later, another 599 tickets were accounted for.[24] As at the first performance in Dublin, the association between charity and *Messiah* generated a public success: this seems to have guaranteed future acceptance for the work in London, even when performed in the theatre.

We might expect that Handel's Foundling Hospital performances would basically repeat the musical scheme from Covent Garden, but amendments to the names on Handel's conducting score suggest that there was one important modification. Frasi seems to have dropped out from the cast for one or both performances; some of her movements were allocated to the boy treble, but others distributed elsewhere.[25] The sequence beginning 'He was cut off' reverted, for the first time in performance, to the all-tenor manifestation in which it had been composed. 'How beautiful are the Feet' was recomposed for Guadagni (36b/38ii/34b): this was the last new setting that Handel wrote for *Messiah*.

The subsequent history of *Messiah* performances under Handel is straightforward. Adaptations to meet the circumstances of casts year by year were made by re-allocating movements and by a few transpositions. In 1751 Handel's plans for his oratorio season were dislocated, first by his own failing eyesight and then by the death of the Prince of Wales, which closed the theatres before the point in the programme at which he normally presented *Messiah*; but he gave two performances at the Foundling Hospital after Easter to a combined audience of 2,000. In 1752 Handel gave two performances at Covent Garden during Holy Week, and one at the Foundling Hospital after Easter. In 1753 Handel's last Covent Garden performance of *Messiah* was given a week before Good Friday, probably reflecting a change of policy by the theatre management against performances in Holy Week. Thereafter Handel finished his season at the same time every year with one or two performances of *Messiah* (three in 1758–9), followed by an annual performance after Easter at the Foundling Hospital.

1754–1759: Handel's last years

1754 marks an important divide in the history of *Messiah*. It is no accident that the first of several lists of performers, with records of their payments, appears in the Foundling Hospital Minutes for 1754: at this point Handel's blindness prevented him from dealing at first hand with the Hospital, and henceforth arrangements were made through the agency of John Christopher Smith the younger. The extent to which Handel took an active part in subsequent performances is uncertain.[26] He was normally present, and may have exercised some control over artistic matters. Although the dates and organisation of subsequent performances were negotiated through Smith, as late as 1758 the Hospital minutes still referred to the performances as being 'under the direction of Mr. Handel'.[27] In 1759 Handel died between the *Messiah* performance that closed his theatre season on 6 April and the Foundling Hospital performance on 3 May: the Covent Garden performance of *Messiah* was the last time that the composer heard his own music.[28] In musical content, the performances after 1753 seem to have changed little – hardly surprisingly, in view of Handel's disability. The score had in fact been fossilising gradually since 1750. The 'Guadagni' versions of 'But who may abide?' and 'Thou art gone up on high', and the 1745 settings of 'Rejoice greatly' and 'Their sound is gone out', seem to have displaced the previous settings entirely, and the only significant variations lay in the alternation between the soprano and alto settings of 'How beautiful are the feet' and 'If God is for us'. Basically the same version was revived from year to year, in the theatre and at the Foundling Hospital, with minor re-allocation to suit variations in the team of soloists. This explains why the material copied in 1759 and presented to the Hospital under the terms of Handel's will seems to reflect the 1754 performances: it was probably copied from a set of part-books that had been re-used with little alteration over the five-year period.

Handel's intention to bequeath a set of performing material to the Foundling Hospital may have been the source of an unfortunate misunderstanding in 1754. Handel had made his will in 1750, and his thoughts no doubt turned further to the long-term fate of his property as his blindness increased. If Handel mentioned that he intended to provide the Hospital with performing materials to facilitate the continuance of annual presentations of *Messiah* after his death, the Hospital's committee misunderstood his intention and thought that they had been offered exclusive rights over the work itself:

This Committee being informed by the Treasurer of Mr Handel's kind intention to this Charity, of securing his Oratorio of Messiah to the Hospital, and that it should be performed nowhere else, excepting for his own Benefit: and the Treasurer also acquainting them that he had been informed by Mr. Handel, That a Copy had been procured from Ireland, with an Intention that ye same should be performed for the Benefit of other Persons

Resolved

That a letter be wrote to Mr. Handel in the Name of this Committee, to return him Thanks for his kind Intention to this Charity; and to assure him, that they will join with him in such Measures as he shall think most proper to secure to the Charity his very valuable benefaction and to prevent his property from being unjustly invaded by any Person whatsoever.

And this Committee are of Opinion That an Act of Parliament should be applied for, to secure this Benefaction of Mr. Handel's, or any other of the like nature, to the sole use & Benefit of this Hospital.[29]

The Hospital duly drafted a petition to Parliament, but when it was put to the composer, 'the same did not seem agreeable to Mr. Handel for the Present'.[30] Although Handel may have been temporarily offended by the incident, it does not seem to have affected his long-term goodwill towards the Hospital. His bequest of a score and parts of *Messiah* to the Hospital was made in the third codicil to his will in August 1757.[31] The composer's concern about the preservation of his own rights to *Messiah* may however in some way have influenced a further delay in the printed *Songs in Messiah*, which were prepared c.1751–3 but not issued until after Handel's death.[32]

Handel's revisions: aesthetic choice or practical necessity?

While many of Handel's revisions and re-compositions to *Messiah* can be accounted for superficially by the practical needs of the moment – the strengths or deficiencies of the available soloists, or the balance of voices in Handel's casts from year to year – they nevertheless raise aesthetic issues. To what extent did revisions 'improve' the work? Why did Handel not return in later years to some of his earliest settings, such as Mrs Clive's 'But lo, the angel of the Lord' or the duet-and-chorus setting of 'How beautiful are the feet'? While we can never be completely certain of Handel's motives, and while it is not possible to compartmentalise his revisions between expediency and artistic intention (the first inevitably has some effect on the second), we can nevertheless examine the re-balancing of the music involved with successive revisions and see the effects that were produced or modified.

The early revisions

The easiest revisions to deal with are cuts within movements, made early in the work's history and never, so far as we know, restored in subsequent performances. The abbreviations to 'Rejoice greatly' and 'O death, where is thy sting' probably preceded the first performance: it looks as if Handel decisively rejected the sprawl of his original compositions and, unless we wish to perform *Messiah* 'as first imagined by the composer', there seems little reason to restore the original versions (–/A7/16a and –/A15/44).[33] The same might be said for 'Why do the nations'. Handel's replacement of more than half the original aria (bars 37–96 in version 38a/40i/36) with a nine-bar recitative (producing 38/40ii/36x) looks at first sight like a concession to the modest skills of the bass soloist in Dublin. The recitative ending replaced not merely the 'B' section of the aria (whose text it carried), but half the 'A' section as well, which it interrupted dramatically at the 'binary-dominant' cadence. Subsequent sources relating directly to Handel's performances all suggest that he retained the short ending. It is reasonable to conclude, therefore, that Handel came to prefer its tightening of the drama between 'Why do the nations' and 'Let us break their bonds asunder'. If subsequent bass soloists felt aggrieved at losing part of the original aria (unlikely, since the original probably never appeared in their part-books), Handel would no doubt have responded that the bass's big moment was not here but in Part Three, with 'The trumpet shall sound'.

The course of one other simple abbreviation is more difficult to chart. In the composition autograph, Handel first wrote an eleven-bar *Pifa*, and then extended it with a new central section (at which he made two attempts[34]) to form a full *da capo* movement of thirty-two bars. Secondary sources suggest that Handel performed this longer form at the earliest performances, but that during the 1750s (and by 1754 at the latest) he returned to the original eleven-bar form. It is difficult to date the rescension, and still more difficult to guess a reason for it. In context the *Pifa* will 'work' in either form, and the cut produces a saving of time barely significant within the work as a whole. For the moment our 'best guess' is to date the shortening of the *Pifa* to the revisions of 1750, and to regard the longer variant as standard for Handel's earlier performances.

An equally difficult, and musically more significant, question surrounds the various settings of 'How beautiful are the feet' and 'Their sound is gone out'. The reasons for Handel's substitution of the Isaiah text in the duet-and-chorus version before the first performance, apparently without consulting the librettist, remain obscure. He probably recognised that his treatment of 'Their sound is gone out' as the 'B' section of the original *da capo* aria 'How beautiful are the feet' (–/A13/34a) was weak, neither projecting the text well nor giving a dramatically satisfactory return to the opening text. The transition from 'How beautiful are the feet' (duet) into 'Break forth into joy' (chorus) in the Dublin movement produces exactly the sort of transition achieved, probably at Jennens's insistence, when in 1745 he added the chorus setting of 'Their sound is gone out' to the A section of his original (Romans text) aria. In his 1743 London performances Handel seems to have been guided by his attachment to the duet-and-chorus composed for Dublin, after which another chorus for 'Their sound is gone out' would not have been effective: hence he chose to add a short aria setting of 'Their sound is gone out' when (as we may suppose) Jennens insisted on that text being reinstated. The substitution of the Isaiah-text duet-and-chorus in 1742 and 1743 is so radical that it must have been based on some aesthetic choice which is now difficult to fathom. So perhaps it is best to take Handel on trust, and regard the 1742–3 versions of *Messiah* as entities that should be performed whole or not at all.

Handel's later revisions and the 1750 version

Handel seems subsequently to have taken a different stylistic view of some sections of the oratorio. The 'Guadagni' settings of 'But who may abide' and 'Thou art gone up on high' are in a subtly later style and make uneasy bedfellows with the 1742–3 sequences of 'How beautiful are the feet', Mrs Clive's version of 'But lo, the angel of the Lord', or the compound-time setting of 'Rejoice greatly'; it is perhaps not surprising that Handel dropped the earlier settings entirely in his later performances.[35] This is not to imply that, as a whole, the 1750s scheme is 'better' than the earlier ones, though individual movements may be preferred: rather, the successive, apparently peripheral changes to *Messiah* add up to two distinctly different musical balances between the versions of 1742–3 and 1750.

The path towards the 1750 version was set in 1745 when, presumably at Jennens's suggestion or insistence, two important revisions were undertaken: composition of the chorus 'Their sound is gone out' as a companion-piece to the shortened aria 'How beautiful are the feet' (36/38i/34ax), and recomposition of 'Rejoice greatly' into the common-time version Handel always performed thereafter. The structure of the short-

ened compound-time version of 'Rejoice, greatly' (16a/18ii/16ax) was
carried forward exactly to the new one: Handel added new violin and voice
parts above a bass line from the old version prepared by a copyist. The
reason for this revision is not hard to guess. The end of Part One was
lacking in variety, with successive movements in B flat major, the first two
of which were for soprano soloist and in 12/8 time (though at different
tempi). Handel had introduced some variety into the scheme before the first
performance by re-allocating 'He shall feed his flock' to contralto, and at
various later revivals he divided the movement between contralto and
soprano.[36] The re-metrification of 'Rejoice, greatly' introduces more
variety into the last 'scene' of Part One, preserving the compound rhythm
only for 'He shall feed his flock', throwing into relief its pastoral symbolism
here and in the *Pifa*. If the initiative for this revision came from Jennens, it
certainly speaks well for his musical sensitivity.

Handel's last major revisions, the 'Guadagni' versions of 1750, focused
once again on two movements that had already engaged his attention. The
original bass version of 'But who may abide?' (5b/A2/6a) had been
amended and transposed for tenor for the London performances of 1743:
although the full details of this revision cannot be recovered with certainty,
Handel's alterations to the autograph and conducting score show that he
realised that the effect of the aria's second part would be improved if the
melismatic treatment of the 'refiner's fire' was heard once only.[37] It is
uncertain which version was performed in 1745 and 1749: the 1749
word-book shows it as a recitative, but this may have been an error carried
over from the Dublin 1742 word-book. In 1750, Handel searched out
suitable openings in the score for revisions that would make their mark
musically but would not upset the balance of the surrounding movements.
He probably perceived the original bass aria as being rather in his 'old'
style, and also saw the opportunity for a different musical treatment of the
'refiner's fire'.[38] The unity originally provided by giving the aria and its
preceding *accompagnato* recitative to the same singer had already been
broken when Handel re-allocated the aria to tenor in 1743: in any case, the
text gave the hint for a voice-change between the prophecy of the
accompagnato and the 'reaction' of the aria. Handel's 1750 setting sig-
nificantly shifts the musical weight of the scene. The longer aria naturally
attracts attention to itself, in contrast to the recessive original setting which
more clearly led on towards the chorus as the climax of the musical group;
but the new aria is not so extensive as to hinder the thread of the dramatic
argument.

The other aria selected for attention in 1750 was 'Thou art gone up on high', on which Handel had also made two attempts already. The original bass aria (34a/36ii/32a), which may have been performed in Dublin, was replaced in the first London performances by a setting for soprano (34b/A10/32b).[39] The text gave little opportunity for dramatic contrasts or illustrative setting, and Handel sensibly concentrated on musical-rhetorical 'argument'. It is difficult to judge which version comes off best: each contains some good ideas that are not in the others.

While Handel's 'Guadagni' settings of these arias are at least on a par with their predecessors, the case for his alto setting of 'How beautiful are the feet' (36b/38ii/34b) is more uncertain. It is musically adequate, and sufficiently different from its soprano progenitor to justify occasional inclusion, but it lacks the sense of urgent creative energy apparent in the other two new arias. Perhaps it was turned out quickly between performances in 1750, though other examples show that Handel could produce some of his best work under pressure. The strongest argument for using the aria in performance would arise from circumstances close to those for which it was originally written: a team of soloists noticeably stronger in the alto department than in the soprano.

Versions for modern performances

In modern performances, my own inclination is to avoid mixing 'early' and 'late' versions. Handel's post-'Guadagni' scheme of 1750 (or one of its later variations) makes one good plan, and cases could be made out for performances based on early schemes from Dublin (1742) or London (1743): but a brew with elements from each is usually unsatisfactory. If we have confidence in Handel's judgement, then the best course is to pursue the plan of one of his performances in its entirety. The musical features of individual schemes are varied, but they may cut across other practical constraints: a choir seeking an unusual version for its annual *Messiah* performance might decide to attempt the 1742 or 1743 versions, for example, but could immediately defeat the purpose of the enterprise by engaging only four soloists.

The best match with one of Handel's versions may be achieved by considering the circumstances which produced a particular scheme. If several 'Cathedral'-type soloists are available, then the 1742 version may be most appropriate: if only four soloists are employed, then one of the later schemes is better. If two soprano voices are used, Handel's second

1743 scheme may be considered, or that of 1749, or the Foundling Hospital scheme of 1754.[40] If two altos are available, one of the schemes from 1750 demands first consideration. Handel's distribution of the music between soprano and boy treble, and between contralto and male alto, provides a lead to the allocation of music between solo voices in the same register but with different timbres: this will be helpful when two sopranos or two contraltos are involved, as well as when using a boy treble or male alto. (Few performances will come so close to Handel's as to include an alto castrato.)

Handel's revisions, beyond his few initial abbreviations, provide no defensive ammunition for wholesale cuts in *Messiah*. The nineteenth-century practice, reinforced by footnotes and musical appendices in some vocal scores, of cutting 'Thou art gone up on high', the B section of 'The trumpet shall sound' and all the music thereafter until 'Worthy is the Lamb', can be defended neither from the libretto nor the music. The texts of 'Thou art gone up on high' and 'If God be for us' contain theological propositions that Jennens would have regarded as essential to the train of argument about the 'Mystery of Godliness' that forms the subject of *Messiah*. 'The trumpet shall sound' remained the bass soloist's main contribution throughout Handel's performances, always as a full *da capo* or *dal segno* aria; the argument for preserving its integrity is very strong. A cut from 'The trumpet shall sound' to 'Worthy is the Lamb' not only removes essential texts and some good music: it also squashes all of the trumpet-D-major music together into a block, removing the flat-key contrast within Part Three. If you cannot manage all of *Messiah* in one evening, it is better to follow the practice of the subscription concerts at the Oxford Music Room in the 1750s, which spread it over two.

Handel's practice with regard to transposition involves two distinct procedures. The first is the straightforward transposition of movements to a new key to suit a singer of different range. Two arias, for example, were so treated in 1754 to provide a part for a second soprano, and it is significant that this was just when blindness began to limit Handel's activity: previously the transposition of an aria had also normally involved some form of creative re-composition, either entire (alto version of 'How beautiful are the Feet') or in details of the accompaniment (alto version of 'If God be for us'). The second procedure maintained the original key, but subjected the vocal part to octave transposition. Handel seems to have been happy to distribute the sequence of solo movements in Part Two between 'Thy rebuke hath broken his heart' and 'But thou didst not leave', originally for tenor, between soprano, treble and tenor. The only example of wholesale octave transposition occurred in 1743, when a soprano took over a substantial portion of the tenor role, probably in response to a sudden emergency in the cast. The only *downward* octave transposition in Handel's performances came when 'Rejoice greatly' was sung on one occasion by the tenor, almost certainly because the soprano role was being carried by a boy treble alone. The choice of movement is significant: 'Rejoice greatly' is accompanied by *unisoni* violins, and has considerable 'breaks' in which the voice is supported by continuo alone, so the downward transposition did not collide with a full orchestral texture (though there would still have been some uncomfortable inversions between the vocal part and the harmonic bass line). It would distort Handel's intentions to allocate this movement regularly to a tenor today.

Handel's generally careful practice gives no support to random transpositions to suit individual circumstances, which would cut across either his key-sequences or his balanced 'scoring' of the vocal part against the accompanying texture. A particularly bad example, given a false appearance of legitimacy in some nineteenth-century vocal scores, is the downward transposition of the Guadagni 'But who may abide' for bass, presumably to maintain continuity with the preceding recitative. This dumps the original high-range coloratura into the middle of the orchestral texture, where it is both unmusical and ineffective.[41]

5

Messiah in other hands

The Foundling Hospital committee's reference to a score of *Messiah* being procured from Ireland so that the work could be performed 'for the Benefit of other Persons' provides a reminder that several performances were given under other auspices during Handel's lifetime: Handel apparently did not object to this, provided he had given his permission.[1] In Dublin the Charitable Musical Society gave annual performances from 1744,[2] and the score referred to in the Foundling Hospital minute was presumably one that Handel himself had supplied (or left behind) for the Society's use. As early as February 1744, *Messiah* was performed in London by the Academy of Ancient Music at their normal venue, the Crown and Anchor Tavern.[3] In 1749, *Messiah* was performed in the Sheldonian Theatre, Oxford, as part of the musical celebrations accompanying the opening of the Radcliffe Camera:[4] further Oxford performances followed in 1752 and 1754, and then regularly from 1756, either during the University's annual Commemoration of Benefactors or in the programmes of the musical society based at the Holywell Music Room. In 1750 *Messiah* reached Salisbury, with a performance in the New Assembly Room, followed by others in 1752 and 1765. A series of performances in the Bristol and Bath area began in 1755, and *Messiah* entered the repertory of the Three Choirs' Festival in 1757: for the first two years the Festival performances took place in 'secular' buildings as evening concerts, but in 1759 the performance at Hereford took place in the morning at the Cathedral – probably the first performance of *Messiah* in such a building. Once established in festival programmes, particularly if they had charitable financial objects, *Messiah* quickly became a regular annual component. Other provincial centres that saw relatively early performances of *Messiah* were Cambridge (1759), Birmingham (1760), Bury St Edmunds (1760), Liverpool (1766), Newcastle (1778) and Derby (1788).[5]

After 1767, the year in which a full score of *Messiah* was finally published, general access to the music itself ceased to be a problem: before that, performances may have derived from only a handful of manuscript scores. William Hayes, Heather Professor of Music at Oxford between 1741 and 1777, owned one such score (now known, from its later ownership, as the 'Goldschmidt' copy).[6] In addition to directing the performances in Oxford itself, Hayes was variously associated with those at Salisbury, the Three Choirs' Festival, and the short-lived festival in the village of Church Langton, Leicestershire, which began in September 1759.[7] It may be doubted whether many of the performances of *Messiah* mounted by other agencies followed any of the composer's own versions of the oratorio precisely. The main text of the full printed score of 1767 certainly did not reflect the work as performed by Handel from 1750 onwards, since its arias were printed from plates derived from texts that Walsh must have received in 1743 or soon after.

While it is true that performances of *Messiah* spread quickly outside the composer's immediate circle within a few years of Handel's death, a certain continuity from his own performances was preserved in London. Smith the younger continued Handel's series of performances at the Foundling Hospital until 1768, and at Covent Garden Theatre until 1774. The Foundling Hospital performances continued under other directors until 1777.[8] A subtle change of musical emphasis came in 1771, when the financial accounts of the Foundling Hospital performance record that thirty professional chorus singers (twelve trebles, five altos, six tenors, seven basses) were supplemented by '26 Chorus Singers Volunteers not paid'. For the first time singers began to outnumber the orchestra, and the total number of performers crept upwards.

The two performances of *Messiah* at the 'Commemoration of Handel' at Westminster Abbey in 1784 multiplied the performers to such an extent that the work became a different musical experience. Though it is difficult to ascertain precise numbers, *Messiah* was rendered on these occasions by about 500, approximately equally divided between singers and instrumentalists.[9] The Commemoration performances raised a considerable amount of money for the Fund for the Support of Decay'd Musicians, a charity of which Handel had been a founder member and to which he left a generous bequest; it was for the support of professional musicians and their families, and the performers in 1784 seem to have been drawn largely from those of professional status, including lay clerks from ecclesiastical establishments.

The nineteenth century

The magnitude and general style of the Commemoration set the tone for the large festival performances of the nineteenth century in which amateur singers increasingly took part. The spread of musical literacy (partly through the tonic sol-fa movements), allied with the production of cheap vocal scores, brought choral singing within the range of many more performers.[10] The use of vocal scores was in itself something of a practical revolution: Handel's singers, like his orchestral players, had performed from single-line part-books. Amateur or semi-professional choral singers formed the backbone of the performers for the provincial festivals that expanded in the nineteenth century in parallel with the construction of the large town halls. *Messiah* attained and retained its strong hold on festival programmes: often it was the only 'classic' work to be performed complete.

In London, the formation of an amateur choral society in 1833, the Sacred Harmonic Society, held the key to the future. In 1836 the Society determined to abandon programmes of miscellaneous selections and to concentrate on complete oratorios, beginning with *Messiah*. The Society had not participated in the 1834 Commemoration of Handel, which was 'professionally' organised, but the situation was revolutionised in a series of performances at the Crystal Palace, culminating in the Handel Commemoration of 1859. Following the lead of the Sacred Harmonic Society, amateur singers took over *Messiah*: performers were numbered in thousands and audiences in tens of thousands. The foundations were thus laid for the triennial Handel Festivals at Crystal Palace that continued into the twentieth century.

Although our image of *Messiah* performances between 1855 and 1920 is inevitably dominated by the serried ranks of the spectacular festivals, there were certainly many more smaller-scale performances, accompanied by organ or an *ad hoc* orchestra, arranged by smaller choral societies and the flourishing choirs of churches and chapels, and geographically distributed throughout Britain. Choruses or sections of *Messiah* were also extracted for liturgical use in church as anthems or motets, a trend that had started in cathedral part-books a century before, possibly even before Handel's death. The 'Hallelujah' chorus as a separate item had appeared in London's charity services as early as 1758.[11]

Additional accompaniments

The change in the aural 'image' of *Messiah* that came about in the nineteenth century involved orchestral sound as well as choral weight. The musical directors of the large festivals normally hired an orchestra for the duration of the programme, and specially-commissioned works by (for example) Sullivan or Dvořák naturally employed the full resources of the contemporary symphony orchestra. For the festival *Messiah* performances, those instruments that were currently available but had not been part of Handel's score – flutes, clarinets, trombones, bass drum – were not left idle.

A distinction must be made between 'strengthening' and strictly 'additional' accompaniments: the former in some way consistently follow the music of Handel's score, while the latter involve some compositional change, either through varying the consistency of the scoring or through alterations and additions to Handel's harmony. Handel himself had added 'strengthening' parts to *Messiah*: oboes and bassoons joined his performances from 1745 (if not before).[12] By 1754 the Foundling Hospital accounts reveal the presence of french horns as well, probably doubling the trumpet parts in the final choruses of Parts Two and Three. It seems very probable that the orchestral accompaniments to the 1784 Commemoration performances were also expanded on the 'strengthening' principle, with oboes, horns and bassoons following something like Handel's practice (though in much greater numbers), the same principles being extended to the double bassoon and the four sets of timpani.[13] At the second *Messiah* performance of the 1784 Commemoration trombones were also added, probably doubling the lower voice parts, and possibly assisting the bass line in the movements where horns were also employed.[14]

A very different path was followed in continental Europe in performances directed by Johann Adam Hiller in Berlin in 1786 and by Mozart in Vienna in 1789. Both adapted Handel's music to the artistic conventions of the current 'classical' orchestra, involving some colouristic use of wind instruments that was removed from Handel's own orchestral style.[15] Mozart's arrangement is naturally of independent interest.[16] His source, a reprint of the English full score of 1767, controlled his choice of variant movements, as well as supplying a few corrupt readings in musical details. The words were translated into German, but Mozart generally preserved Handel's vocal lines and string parts, adding parts for flutes, oboes, clarinets, bassoons, horns, trombones, trumpets and timpani. The rewriting of Handel's trumpet parts was enforced by the change in players' techniques; the trumpets in 1789 were middle-register fanfare instruments, and the employment of the higher *clarino* register was both unsafe and unfashionable. Complete recomposition of 'The trumpet shall sound' was needed not only because of the technical problems posed by Handel's trumpet obbligato part, but also because in the German Bibles another instrument (the 'posaune') signalled the general resurrection accompanying judgement day. Mozart also recomposed 'If God be for us' as an accompanied recitative, with the approval of Gottfried van Swieten who described Handel's original aria as 'cold'.[17] More controversially, Mozart filled out Handel's sparse string textures in movements such as 'The people that walked in darkness' and 'Thou shalt break them' with exotic wind harmonies. As an interesting, and sometimes moving, experience of the coalescence of two great musical minds, Mozart's version of *Messiah* remains worth performing, but it needs to be taken complete, and the circumstances of the Viennese performance that defined various artistic decisions preclude a sensible 'English' version of Mozart's score. Some fifteen to twenty years later, Beethoven showed a different sort of creative interest in *Messiah*, copying fragments into his sketch-books.[18] During his first visit to London, Haydn attended the Handel Commemoration of 1791 at Westminster Abbey: his own later oratorios were stimulated by this experience.

'Mozart's *Messiah*' was published in Leipzig in 1803, in a version that included elements from Hiller's arrangement, and in nineteenth-century Britain this score became fair game for further arrangement. Influential, too, was Robert Franz's 'completion' of Mozart's score, published in 1885. It is rather ironic, and a sure indicator of the continuing demand for 'festival' versions, that Ebenezer Prout's edition of *Messiah* published in 1902 combined a conscious attempt to re-establish the minutiae of Handel's music with a full score that was reluctant to withdraw 'additional accompaniments': a few of these are printed in small type for use 'only in the absence of an organ', but most are not distinguished from Handel's own contribution.

To the present day

Although the social changes accompanying the First World War attenuated the choral festival tradition to which 'additional accompaniments' were practically relevant, *Messiah* remained resilient in both 'small' and 'large' guises as a part of the living musical repertory of Britain. Events took an unexpected turn in the 1960s with a fashion for 'sing-in' performances with minimum specific rehearsal, thus reviving the large-scale *Messiah* that had otherwise seemed to be a thing of the past. In general, however, modern festival performances are not on a scale that positively demands additional accompaniments and the choice usually falls on a strengthened version of Handel's own scoring. To the exasperation of many a choral conductor, the vocal scores of Prout, and even of Vincent Novello, remain in use among devoted choralists, along with more modern texts.

By the time Prout's edition was published, trends towards a closer re-examination of Handel's own versions of *Messiah*, and towards performances of an 'authentic' type, were already under way. The publication of a facsimile of Handel's composition autograph by the Sacred Harmonic Society in 1868, and of a booklet concentrating on textual details of the score by the Master of the Queen's Music (who had care of the autograph scores in the Royal Library) in 1874,[19] show that *Messiah*'s popularity was inducing an interest in its original form and circumstances. By the 1890s, the conflict between the sight of Handel's score and the sound of the festival performances was producing a strong reaction. It is interesting to compare George Bernard Shaw's reviews of festival performances in 1877 and 1891.[20] The first concentrates mainly on technical details of the performance, while the second concludes:

> Why, instead of wasting huge sums on the multitudinous dullness of a Handel Festival does not somebody set up a thoroughly rehearsed and exhaustively studied performance of the Messiah in St James's Hall with a chorus of twenty capable artists? Most of us would be glad to hear the work seriously performed once before we die.

By 1894 Arthur Henry Mann had taken up the challenge with a performance of *Messiah* in the chapel of King's College, Cambridge. In order to produce a performance as close to the circumstances of Handel's as possible – in its combination of variant movements, and in the size and composition of the orchestra and choir – Mann sought out all available *Messiah* sources: the rediscovery of the Foundling Hospital score and performing material seems to have been made at his instigation.[21] In combining scholarship with a practical intent, Mann may be regarded as the father of modern *Messiah* studies: his papers and annotated score[22] reveal that he had subjected the sources to extensive and coherent interpretation that must command the admiration of a modern *Messiah* scholar. By contrast, Prout's score of 1902 seems retrogressive; the *Händelgesellschaft* score published in the same year had much more to commend it.[23]

Mann's lead was not much taken up during the next half-century. The deposit of the Royal Music Library at the British Museum in the 1920s by King George V made some important *Messiah* sources (including the composition autograph) more accessible, and Handel scholarship was maintained mainly by two custodians of the Museum collection, William

Barclay Squire and W. C. Smith. Smith's important study of the earliest printed editions of *Messiah* was the most significant contribution to new literature on the work during the inter-war period.[24]

With the 1950s, however, interest in *Messiah* entered a new and exciting phase. Several factors contributed to this – the introduction of well-organised music study courses at British universities, the increased availability of the sources (the Royal Music Library was presented outright to the nation by Queen Elizabeth II in 1957) and the advent of the long-playing record. While some of the new complete three-disc performances of *Messiah* preserved the old-style presentation,[25] a new direction was taken by a performance in March 1950 at St Paul's Cathedral by the London Choral Society conducted by John Tobin. Tobin had made an attempt to establish a good text for *Messiah* and returned to Handel's scoring, though the proportions of his performing forces were naturally controlled by the institutional framework of the London Choral Society and were not reduced to the size employed by Handel.[26] While instrumentations and speeds became more 'authentic' in the next generation of performances and recordings,[27] experiments were also made with ornamentation based on a wide interpretation of eighteenth-century performance treatises: in retrospect, Tobin's heavily-drilled chorus ornamentation and extensive aria cadenzas now seem out of place, though they reflect an outlook of healthy and necessary experimentation.

Handel scholarship revived dramatically, in the approach to the Handel anniversary of 1959, with Winton Dean's monumental study of Handel's other oratorios (*Handel's Dramatic Oratorios and Masques*) and O. E. Deutsch's *Documentary Biography* of the composer. A more specialised 'Messiah industry' suddenly took up the study of the work in earnest.[28] The foundations of modern *Messiah* scholarship were laid in a book (*'Messiah': Origins, Compositions, Sources*) by Jens Peter Larsen in 1957 and in the performing edition by Watkins Shaw (1959) followed by an accompanying book (*A Textual and Historical Companion to Handel's 'Messiah'*) which presented an extended guide to sources and matters of textual authority, as well as a reconstruction of the historical framework for Handel's performances. Tobin's edition was also published, with accompanying books about *Messiah*, though it has to be admitted that they appear rather disorganised and old-fashioned in outlook when set against Shaw's work.[29] The independent work of two American scholars is worthy of record: the editions of J. M. Coopersmith (1946) and Alfred Mann (1961) were both based on fresh consideration of sources.

The more recent history of *Messiah* has been dominated by the establishment of professional 'Baroque' orchestras using period (or replica) instruments played in the appropriate manner. Although it will no doubt appear in time that this phenomenon was connected with some musical need of the later 1970s, the thoroughgoing application of historical and aural imagination to *Messiah* was long overdue. The successful 'authentic' recording of the 1754 Foundling Hospital version of *Messiah*, released in 1980, will surely form as important a landmark in the history of the work's performances as Shaw's edition.[30] The movement from performances such as A. H. Mann's that employed numerical performing strengths comparable with Handel's, to performances that also try to recreate the sound of his orchestra and employ musicians attempting to approach the work with the same attitudes as their eighteenth-century counterparts, is directed not merely through antiquarian curiosity, but from a desire to come closer to an understanding of the work itself. Such an understanding can only be beneficial to performances of *Messiah* in other circumstances.

6

Design

Messiah within the oratorio genre

Messiah was created within the specific genre of Handel's London theatre oratorios, and against a background of experience built up by both composer and audience prior to 1741. The theatre audience's expectation of a three-section evening's entertainment, lasting about three hours in performance with two intervals, was carried over from the three acts of Italian opera to the three parts of English oratorio. The perceived characteristics of Handel's oratorios were neatly summed up by Newburgh Hamilton in his Preface to the printed libretto for *Messiah*'s 'twin' oratorio, *Samson*:

> Mr. *Handel* happily introduc'd here *Oratorios*, a musical Drama, whose Subject must be Scriptural, and in which the Solemnity of Church-Musick is agreeably united with the most pleasing Airs of the Stage.[1]

Even so, we may still be slightly surprised by Jennens's description of *Messiah* as 'a fine Entertainment'.[2]

Three features set *Messiah* apart from the main body of Handel's oratorios. The text, adapted from scripture (the Authorised Version of the Bible and the 'Coverdale' translation of the psalms associated with the Book of Common Prayer), includes no metrical or rhymed verse, such as was normally characteristic of aria texts for opera and oratorio. While the prose 'verses' of the scriptural sources have no metrical structure, they do nevertheless have a controlled rhetorical flow: English translations of the scriptures were, after all, intended as 'performance texts', to be read aloud at public worship. Their measured sentences frequently divide into balanced clauses (synonymous, constructive or antithetic) delineated by a colon or semi-colon. Secondly, the text is presented in narrative format, with no impersonation of dramatic characters: this is in direct contrast to *Samson*, where individual singers represented Samson, Dalila, Harapha and Manoa. Furthermore, the narrative function in *Messiah* is not concentrated in one voice: the 'story' is carried forward by soloists and chorus, though in Handel's first composition score the tenor received a slightly enhanced role as principal narrator for Part Two, a feature perhaps influenced by the tenor/evangelist of the German Passion.[3] There are a few instances of directly reported speech: the prophecy in 'Thus saith the Lord'; the words of the angel and angel-host when they appear to the shepherds; the mockery of the crowd in 'He trusted in God'; and an ironic use of reported speech at 'Unto which of the Angels'. But mostly the story-line is presented obliquely: soloists and chorus are identified less with participants in the drama than with the faithful believers who receive and acclaim the 'Mystery of Godliness' that Jennens identified as the oratorio's theme. The scriptural 'prose' text and the narrative (rather than 'dramatised') presentation were anticipated in one previous oratorio of Handel's – *Israel in Egypt* from 1738–9 – whose libretto, as already noted, may also have been Jennens's work. The technique of narrative presentation also has some ancestry in the odes previously set by Handel, in particular *Alexander's Feast* and *L'Allegro*.

The aspect that most sets *Messiah* apart from all of Handel's other English oratorios, however, is its subject-matter. In *La Resurrezione* and the *Brockes Passion*, Handel had dealt with incidents from the life of Christ, but these works were written for, and performed in, traditions very different from those of the London theatres. In bringing a 'Sacred Oratorio' into the programme of the regular theatres, even during the Lenten period, Handel took a risk. It is doubtful whether he lost any regular patrons as a result of performing *Messiah* in 1743, but the controversy surrounding the first London performances would have been stressful: it came in any case at a difficult time, when Handel was already resisting pressures from the new Italian opera company and was probably feeling increasingly sensitive about audience reactions to his performances.

Ten years later *Messiah* had, unpredictably, turned from a liability into an asset with London audiences. This may largely be attributed to the successful association between *Messiah* and the charitable objects of the Foundling Hospital, which cancelled out the puritan scruples voiced in 1743. It is likely also that Handel's audience had changed somewhat in character by the mid-1750s: the gloss of high aristocratic patronage that had been the legacy from Italian opera may have been replaced by a solid middle-class audience with a more serious outlook. By then, attendance at 'Mr Handel's Oratorios' may have become a tradition in itself, almost a work of virtue for Lent: if so, *Messiah* would have been the natural culmination to a subscriber's season.[4] With *Messiah*, Handel may have

accidentally anticipated the character of his future audience: the tempera-
ment and outlook of the audience for the first Dublin performances in
1742 was probably closer to this London audience of the 1750s than to its
strictly contemporary London counterpart. While *Messiah*'s subject-matter
seems to have been generally acceptable to the Dublin audience, in
London it had to wait on the development of charitable associations and a
change in audience attitudes. And this was in spite of the fact that Handel
and his librettist had clearly differentiated the manner in which the story
was presented from that of more conventional dramatic oratorios.

After *Messiah*, only one of Handel's later English oratorios bears any
similarity in its manner of presentation: *The Triumph of Time and Truth*, first
produced in 1757. This was, however, an 'englished' version of *Il Trionfo
del Tempo*, and cannot legitimately be regarded as an advance or development on *Messiah*: rather the reverse, in fact, since the structure was old (as
was most of the music), and the balance of new creative input between
Handel and the younger John Christopher Smith is questionable.[5] In the
end, *Messiah* stands alone within the sub-genre of oratorio that Handel
created with his English theatre works: no other oratorio had subject-
matter that necessitated exactly the same treatment.

The libretto: structure and content

Jennens organised his libretto within the framework of the conventional
Three Parts. Part One deals with prophecies concerning the Saviour, and
their fulfilment in his incarnation; Part Two charts the course of events
from Christ's passion to the final triumph of his second coming; Part
Three is an extended commentary on Christ's role as Saviour. The 1743
word-book, which must be assumed to have had Jennens's authority, further
divides the Parts into numbered sections comparable to operatic scenes.
The subjects of Jennens's 'scenes' are as follows:

Part One: I Isaiah's prophecy of Salvation: the Gospel or 'good news';
II The judgement that will accompany the appearance of the Saviour;
III The specific prophecy of Christ's birth; IV The Incarnation,
announced to the shepherds near Bethlehem; V; The redemption and
healing brought by the Saviour.

Part Two: I Christ's passion, scourging and crucifixion; II Christ's
death and resurrection; III Christ's ascension; IV Christ's reception in
Heaven; V Whitsun, and the subsequent preaching of the Gospel; VI The
world's hostile reception to the Gospel; VII God's ultimate victory.

Part Three: I The promise of eternal life and the triumph over Original

Sin, through Christ's victory; **II** The general resurrection that will accompany the Day of Judgement; **III** The final conquest over sin; **IV** Acclamation of the Messiah.

A number of things are striking about the way that Jennens followed through his scheme. Part Two 'scene' II receives surprisingly little emphasis, presumably because the general theme of resurrection figures so largely in Part Three.[6] The chain of events in Part Two is narrated so obliquely, through allusive biblical references carrying very little direct description, that it would be incomprehensible to an audience without prior knowledge of the subject: the listener must be, if not necessarily a believer, at least well versed in the scriptural accounts of events between Maundy Thursday and Whit Sunday, and needs to know something of their conventional theological interpretation. Apart from the symbolic references in Part One 'scene' V, there is no treatment of Christ's teaching or pastoral ministry between his Incarnation and his Passion. Jennens pays almost no attention to what Jesus said or did, because *Messiah* is not about these things: the subject of the drama is God's redemption of mankind through the Messiah, and the conflicts involved are viewed from cosmic and eternal perspectives. The texts that Jennens chose as the mottoes for the title page of the word-book not only summarise the subject of the oratorio, but also provide the signal that it is not going to be a normal 'human drama'.

Given Jennens's frame of reference, his eclectic selection of allusive biblical texts is remarkably effective. The hand of the dramatist is most apparent in his employment of appropriate Old Testament texts to portray the transition from Resurrection to Whitsun in Part Two, and the world's hostile reception to the gospel in Part Two 'scenes' VI–VII. In using Old and New Testament texts to illuminate each other, Jennens sometimes went beyond interpretations that were strictly defensible from the New Testament alone.[7] In his choice and combination of texts, Jennens may have been influenced by the lectionary of the Book of Common Prayer, which linked Old Testament lessons to Christian festivals and seasons throughout the church's year.[8] According to one report Jennens 'read prayers [presumably using the liturgies of Morning and Evening Prayer from the Book of Common Prayer] to his family daily' in his private chapel at Gopsal.[9] He clearly had an intimate knowledge of the scriptures and a jackdaw-like mind for picking out and storing texts that suited his purpose. Although detailed theological considerations are beyond the scope of this book, there can be little doubt that Jennens had a specific 'purpose' behind his selection of texts: they support and promote a particular interpretation of Jesus as the Messiah, and assert partisan views about the Resurrection and Redemption from Sin in a period when Anglicans of Jennens's orthodox cast found themselves in theological conflict with Deists and Free-thinkers.[10]

It is also difficult to resist the impression that the view of the conflict between the Gospel and the world's power-structures portrayed in Part Two 'scenes' VI–VII was coloured by Jennens's own sense of persecution as an Anglican non-juror. However, Jennens drew the bounds of his allusive biblical references in sufficiently broad terms to be acceptable to a wide spectrum of Christian opinion. More important still, Jennens and Handel together created an oratorio which, although dealing primarily with the abstract idea of 'the Messiah', presented a well-known story through a series of musical tableaux whose emotional progressions can still be appreciated by believers and unbelievers alike.

The intention that the text would eventually be set to music clearly affected the structure of Jennens's compilation. The libretto almost certainly came to Handel ready equipped with headings for recitatives, arias and choruses. In arranging Dryden's *Alexander's Feast* for Handel in 1736, Newburgh Hamilton had seen his task as that of making 'a plain Division of it into *Airs, Recitative,* or *Chorus's*',[11] and Jennens's arrangement of the *Messiah* text must have been influenced by the possibilities for such musical opportunities. Handel probably did not diverge far from Jennens's plan: in the course of the performing history of the work, the only major variation in movement-type occurred with 'Their sound is gone out', successively the 'B' section of an aria, omitted completely, recomposed as a short aria, and finally recomposed as a chorus. 'But who may abide?' and 'Thou art gone up on high' may have been set by Handel alternatively as recitatives (though the musical and historical evidence is unsatisfactory), and a similar substitution certainly took place for 'Thou shalt break them'; but such alterations seem to have been made partly from expediency, and were applied to movements that had already been composed as arias to sections of text that Jennens had probably prescribed as such.

While conventional 'theatrical' oratorios naturally proceeded mainly by the opera-derived forms of recitative and aria, bringing in choruses for collective utterance or for commentary on the action, the unusual nature of *Messiah* swung the balance decisively away from recitative. There are no conversations, and the *semplice* recitatives (all short) serve to introduce more substantial arias and choruses. Jennens arranged the texts of most of his 'scenes' to climax with a chorus, usually approached through an ascending sequence of recitative and aria. There is a certain parallel with the design of many of Handel's operas in that the scheme begins in a regular manner, but breaks up under the demands of the 'action'. Part One, which can be regarded as mainly expository, begins with two regular recitative–aria–chorus sequences, followed by a double sequence in 'scene' III. 'Scenes' IV and V follow more fluid designs, but each concludes with a chorus. In the first half of Part Two, the regular sequence-model breaks down completely as the chorus takes on a leading role, providing commentary on a story that is only half-expressed. Although recitative–aria sequences reappear between 'Thy rebuke hath broken his Heart' and 'But Thou didst not leave', the movements themselves are very compressed and it is only with the last 'scene' of Part Two that the regular plan is re-established.[12]

Part Three, although a little more regular than Part Two, nevertheless distributes the relative weights of recitative, aria and chorus in different patterns. Jennens's final 'scene-division' cuts across what might have been a musical aria–chorus sequence. Whether the duet treatment for 'O death, where is thy sting?' was Jennens's idea or Handel's, its placing has a striking parallel with duets in Handel's operas, which frequently occur at the union of a pair of lovers as the plot moves towards resolution. Whatever may have been Jennens's reservations about Handel's musical setting of his text, he must surely have been satisfied with the choruses that ended Parts Two and Three. It is in these choral perorations that *Messiah* presents the strongest contrast to the solo-voice-dominance of opera: the 'airs of the Stage' finally give way to the 'Solemnity of Church-Musick'.

Musical forms in *Messiah*: some general considerations

It in no way diminishes Handel's musical contribution to *Messiah* that he was to some extent writing to the specification of Jennens's libretto: without the background of public theatre oratorio that Handel himself had developed in London during the 1730s, Jennens would in any case not have had the opportunity to create such a work. Even allowing for the probability that Handel followed Jennens's general plan in setting particular movements as arias or choruses, the balance of emphasis between movements, in terms of both length and expressive content, was ultimately controlled by the composer's treatment of the texts. In Part Two, for example, it is Handel who dwells on 'He was despised', but moves fairly briskly through from 'Thy rebuke hath broken his heart' to 'But thou didst not leave his soul in hell'.

As regards expressive content, a rough distinction may be made between movements which are 'text-led' (putting over the emotional message of the text as forcefully as possible) and those which are 'music-led' (setting the text appropriately, but evolving the movement primarily through extension, development and contrast in the musical ideas). The distinction cannot be absolute, for an extended aria or chorus necessarily relies on 'musical' aspects for its continuation. Nevertheless, there is a difference between Handel's 'active' setting of texts such as 'Rejoice greatly' or 'Why do the nations' on the one hand, with their strongly characterised emotions, and the more 'neutral' movements such as 'Thou art gone up on high', 'If God be for us' and 'O Death, where is thy sting?' In the duet, Handel may have decided to concentrate on purely musical development because there was little emotional 'meat' to be gained from the rather obscure final clauses of the text. Since the oratorio was about the *idea* of 'the Messiah', the scheme required a number of abstract texts: by his treatment of these, Handel introduced a variety and equilibrium into the work's musical and dramatic elements. He was not simply making the best of a bad job.

Various external factors apart from the structure of Jennens's libretto influenced or stimulated Handel in the composition of *Messiah*. Although it is likely that *Messiah* was composed to be put 'into the bank' for an oratorio season whose outlines and performers were as yet undefined, Handel was no doubt influenced by the capacities of the soloists, orchestra and chorus singers with whom he had previously worked. While it cannot reasonably be maintained that any of the music in the 1741 composition score was specifically written for John Beard or Susanna Cibber, Handel was well acquainted with the types of performers that they represented. One external factor that certainly had an important effect on the musical scheme was Handel's inclusion of trumpets and drums: this set the closing choruses of Parts Two and Three into D major, the trumpets' best key, and the same key acted as the target for the Incarnation sequence in Part One which ends with 'Glory to God', a chorus employing trumpets without drums.[13] The inclusion of the 'angel trumpets' in 'Glory to God' – the Miltonic association derives from *Samson* – was a carefully calculated effect over which Handel may have been initially rather over-ambitious and impractical. He intended them to be located 'off-stage': in the composition autograph he first wrote 'in disparte' and then altered this to 'da lontano e un poco piano'. But whether through negligence on the part of the copyist or because Handel thought better of the idea, the direction was not copied into the conducting score, nor into any secondary source reflecting Handel's performances. If he still considered the physical location of the trumpets to be important, it is strange that Handel did not write the missing direction into the conducting score himself.

One other external factor seems to have influenced Handel's choice of keys for certain movements. In some movements Handel re-worked thematic material from his secular Italian duets for two voices and basso continuo: 'O Death, where is thy sting' from 'Se tu non lasci amore' (*c.*1722), HWV 193, first movement,[14] 'His yoke is easy' from 'Quel fior che all'alba ride' (completed 2 July 1741), HWV 192, first movement; 'And he shall purify' from 'Quel fior che all'alba ride', last movement;[15] 'For unto us a child is born' from 'Nò, di voi non vo' fidarmi' (completed 3 July 1741), HWV 189, first movement; 'All we, like sheep' from 'Nò, di voi non vo' fidarmi', last movement. Presumably the themes came to Handel as he was reading through Jennens's libretto as suitable in metre and mood for the texts in *Messiah*: most came from recently composed duets, and the melodies would still have been fresh in his memory. (If this was the case, then the self-borrowings present further circumstantial evidence that Handel did not even begin to think about the composition of Jennens's libretto before July 1741.)[16] All but the last-named provided the leading themes for the *Messiah* movements, and all four of these carried their duet keys forward into the oratorio. Even though three of the four were re-worked as choruses, Handel seems to have 'heard' the movements in the keys derived from the duets and structured the surrounding key-relationships in *Messiah* accordingly.

The controlling factors of the keys suitable for trumpets and the key-influence of the movements derived from Italian duets seem to rule out the possibility of any overall tonal scheme for the oratorio, though it is tempting to read such an intention not only into the D major conclusions to Parts Two and Three but also in the possibility that the E major of 'I know that my Redeemer liveth' at the beginning of Part Three may refer back to 'Comfort ye' at the beginning of Part One. But while Handel probably did not work to a strategic plan for tonal centres throughout the whole work, he did nevertheless pay attention to key-variety, key-contrast and key-sequence between movements and scenes. The break-up of the simple recitative–aria–chorus sequences in Part One as the work proceeds is mirrored in a transition towards more flexible tonal schemes. Apart from the Incarnation sequence ('scene' IV), which is (literally) dramatically different, all of the 'scenes' in Part One as composed remain in the same tonal centre for their first two movements:

I   E major – E minor – A major
II D minor – D minor[17] – G minor
III (Recit) – D major aria – D major chorus – B minor – B minor –
     G major
V   B flat major – B flat major[18] – B flat major(!)

Such predictable successions of tonal stability come but rarely as the work progresses. Perhaps coincidentally, the most stable examples are associated with the bass soloist: the C major sequence from 'Why do the Nations' to the chorus 'Let us break their bonds assunder', and the recitative–aria sequence 'Behold, I tell you a mystery' / 'The trumpet shall sound'. The other obvious 'same-key' sequence is between the choruses 'Surely he hath borne our griefs' and 'And with his stripes', but the 1743 word-book prints this as one movement, and Handel may well have regarded it as a two-limbed single chorus.[19] These choruses in any case fall within a 'scene' that is particularly interesting in its overall organisation and deserves consideration as a whole.

Part Two 'scene' I

The first 'scene' of Part Two is dominated by two musical elements: the extensive role assigned to the chorus, and the spacious full *da capo* aria 'He was despised'. A rich blend of possible influences may be detected. While the extensive choral contribution may have been specifically suggested by Jennens's draft libretto, the librettist as well as the composer may have related the musical opportunities of this section of the text to the German Passion tradition, with its crowd (*turba*) choruses. The grand declamatory opening of 'Behold the Lamb of God' owes something to the spirit of the French-style *Ouverture*, appropriately enough as this is the curtain-raiser to the succeeding drama as well as the prelude to the formal Second Part.[20] The key and the extended treatment of 'He was despised', however, seem to derive from Handel's personal schematic preferences: *Samson* has a similarly weighty, yet lyrical, movement in the same key, for a soloist in the same register, in the comparable position near the beginning of Part Two ('Return, O God of Hosts').

In order to deal adequately with the scheme of the opening section of

Table 1. Part Two, 'scenes' ɪ and ɪɪ – Tonal Organisation[a]

	'scene' I	
Behold the Lamb	G minor	
He was despised	E flat major; C minor → G minor; E flat major *da capo*	'Flat-key'
Surely he hath borne	F minor	
And with his stripes	F minor[b]	
All we, like sheep	F major, ending F minor	
All they that see	B flat minor → E flat major	
He trusted in God	C minor	
Thy rebuke	A flat major → B minor (ending *tierce de picardie*)	
Behold, and see	E minor (ending on chord V)	
	'scene' II	'Sharp-key'
He was cut off	B minor → E major	
But thou didst not leave	A major	

[a] The keys are taken from the score 'as composed': Handel normally performed 'He was despised' in the original key, but may have transposed it upwards in 1745 for Francesina.

[b] When first drafting this movement, Handel ended it with a perfect cadence. At an early stage, probably when 'filling up' the score and certainly before the conducting score was copied, he revised the ending to finish on the dominant chord, giving a strong lead towards the following movement.

Part Two, and Handel's treatment of Jennens's text, it is necessary to take in 'scene' II as well as 'scene' I. In one aspect Handel seems to have deliberately eschewed the opportunity for variety. None of the movements is in triple or compound metres: it is almost as if Handel is telling us that serious musical business is done in quadruple metres or *alla breve*. And it is indeed true that, in spite of its minor key, the next triple-time aria ('Thou art gone up on high') comes almost as a moment of relaxation. Nevertheless, Handel can be serious and powerful in triple time, as 'Thou shalt break them' demonstrates. His choice of successive 'even' metres at the beginning of Part Two, varying only the *tempi*, was surely dictated by the need to keep the argument of the drama as sharply focused as possible: while keeping one element stable to indicate the chain of argument, he could introduce variety and dramatic contrast into other elements. The carefully judged variations in the speeds of successive movements, combined with no less carefully judged variations in their relative lengths, set

Ex. 1 (a)   'He was despised', bars 50–51

Ex. 1 (b)   'Surely he hath borne our griefs', bars 1–2

Ex. 1 (c)   'All they that see him', bars 1–3

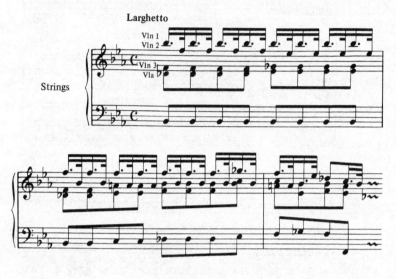

the overall pacing of the first two scenes, and it is from the tonal organisation and occasional motivic clues that we gain an explicit sense of Handel's design.

As may be seen from Table 1, Handel clearly cut across Jennens's scheme: his musical 'first scene' ends with the chorus 'He trusted in God', and the following accompanied recitative provides the transition from the 'flat-key' area of that scene to the 'sharp-key' area of the following three movements. Not only did Handel ignore Jennens's scene-division tonally, he also arranged the music to move from 'Thy rebuke' to 'But thou didst not leave' in a smooth transitional progression, developing the sequence of events through to the resurrection as one unit, and proceeding from minor to major keys.

Within Handel's tonal first scene there are linking cross-relationships, both tonal and thematic, so obvious that they must argue in favour of careful planning. The three central chorus movements form a block in F (minor → minor → major → minor), set within outer landmarks in G minor and C minor/E flat major. In the orchestra the 'smiting' figure from the 'B' section of 'He was despised' recurs at 'Surely he hath borne our griefs', in a context that is one of the most dramatic moments in *Messiah*;[21] it recurs again, this time with more varied pitches and slightly faster, at 'All they that see him' (Ex. 1).

Although Handel divides off the scenes tonally after 'He trusted in God', the progression through the two scenes is carried forward in the ever-widening intervals of the prominent initial *anacruces* of the solo movements: 'He was despised' begins with a rising fourth; in 'All they that see him' and 'Behold and see' the voice entry extends this to a minor sixth and a perfect fifth; and then the interval finally widens to a bright major sixth with the orchestral introduction to 'But thou didst not leave' (Ex. 2).[22]

Ex. 2 (a)   'He was despised'

(b)   'All they that see him'

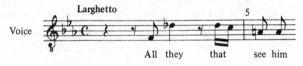

(c)   'Behold and see'

(d)   'but thou didst not leave'

7

Individual movements

Recitatives

The relative insignificance of continuo-accompanied recitatives to Jennens's scheme has already been noted: they are few and short, though they fulil an essential function by introducing new topics that become the subjects of the succeeding arias. Operatic recitatives may sometimes carry considerable emotional weight, at moments of tension or strong feeling that will not bear extension over the longer time-span of an aria. In *Messiah*, the *semplice* recitatives are not used in this way, but some important moments are carried by the orchestrally accompanied ones. In Part One, accompanied recitatives are used when the prophet (metaphorically) raises his voice: 'The voice of him that crieth in the wilderness' and 'Thus saith the Lord'; in Part Two they bear the high-point of the Passion tragedy ('Thy rebuke', 'He was cut off') and introduce the mocking crowd at the Crucifixion ('All they that see him'). Handel's use of the most conventional type of *accompagnato* texture – a sustained wash of string chords – is the more effective by being limited to the Passion recitatives in Part Two and 'Behold, I tell you a mystery' in Part Three. Prophetic moments call forth emphatic rhythmic figures to punctuate the vocal phrases ('The voice of him', 'Thus saith the Lord'), and the same technique proves effective for 'All they that see him' and the revised ending to 'Why do the nations?' Within Part One, however, several *accompagnato* recitatives display strong and continuous metrical tendencies that render them closer to the short arias or *ariosos* that frequently feature near the beginning of acts in Handel's operas. The first part of 'Comfort ye', the whole of 'For behold, darkness shall cover the earth', and the two accompanied recitatives within the nativity sequence are of this type, though all were designated 'accompagnato' by Handel.[1]

Arias

While the *accompagnato* recitatives play an important role in carrying the more dramatic moments of *Messiah*, and while some of the more lyrical movements so designated extend towards the length of short arias ('Behold, darkness shall cover the earth' is actually longer in playing time than 'But thou didst not leave'), nevertheless it is to the longer arias that we must look in order to appreciate the skill and variety with which Handel treated the received musical forms. During the decade preceding *Messiah*, Handel had gradually moved away from reliance on the full *da capo* aria of the Italian operatic tradition.[2] This change is partly attributable to the shift in his interest from Italian opera to the new English genres that he was creating, which did not rely so heavily on the musical habits (and strengths) of the operatic stars: but it also seems likely that Handel's own stylistic choices were moving in the same direction. Nevertheless, all of his major works still included at least one full *da capo* aria, with an opening 'A' section, a contrasted 'B' section and a *reprise* of the 'A' section.[3] In *Messiah*, Handel planned four such arias, spread through the work: 'Rejoice greatly' in Part One;[4] 'He was despised' and 'How beautiful are the feet' (strictly *dal segno*) in Part Two; and 'The trumpet shall sound' in Part Three. They were to be for soprano, alto, soprano and bass respectively: the absence of an extended show-piece aria for tenor is balanced by its heavier narrative role. Perhaps Handel received some suggestions on the subject from Jennens, but if we assume that there was little contact between them during the period of composition, then the selection of these movements for full-scale arias must have been mainly Handel's: 'He shall feed his flock', 'I know that my Redeemer liveth' and 'If God be for us' also had texts susceptible to *da capo* treatment, with opportunities for a contrasted central section and an effective return to the opening, had Handel wished to treat them that way.

Of Handel's four planned *da capo* arias only 'He was despised' survived without some pruning. 'How beautiful are the feet' was rejected before the first performance and the other two were cut down, certainly by 1743 and probably before the first performance. 'The trumpet shall sound' received only minor reduction, becoming a *dal segno* aria by the omission of the introductory ritornello at the reprise: Handel made no internal cuts to the aria itself, nor did he ever perform it in a shortened form. 'Rejoice greatly', however, received radical treatment. In common with many extended *da capo* arias (including the other two major-key ones in *Messiah*), the 'A' section itself was constructed in binary form with two statements of the text, the first cadencing clearly in the dominant key and the second (necessarily) in the tonic. Handel shortened the aria by slicing this 'A' section apart and inserting the 'B' section between the two halves; he made this alteration, which involved re-composing links with the opening and closing tonalities of the 'B' section, in the autograph, possibly while 'filling up' the score.

The 'da capo principle' was also applied by Handel in a disguised form elsewhere, in sequences of movements involving chorus as well. 'Let us break their bonds asunder' stands as the key-equivalent to a reprise of the first section of 'Why do the nations?' The duet-and-chorus version of 'How beautiful are the feet' (36a/[38]/34) took the idea one stage further: at the appropriate point in the chorus (bar 104) Handel brought back the text and melody of the opening theme of the duet.

The variety of aria forms found elsewhere in *Messiah* can best be approached in terms of the interplay between texts and structural/tonal designs. Although many arias may be construed as 'ritornello' forms, moving in musical blocks between related-key cadences that are frequently emphasised or extended by orchestral interludes, the 'binary expectations' within the 'A' section of *da capo* arias may have affected the way that such arias were perceived by the original listeners, hearing the music straight through for the first time without the overall map provided by access to a score. The terms of the musical journey in each aria usually become apparent after the first significant cadence-point, usually in the dominant key (or, for minor-key arias, the relative major). The repetitions of text after the cadence-point in 'Every valley' and 'But thou didst not leave' signal a simple binary movement. The reference to 'light' on the end of both parts of the text of 'The people that walked' suggested a similar binary scheme to Handel, but with a different text in the second half repeating the emotional progression of the first.

In 'Thou art gone up on high' Handel worked to a fundamentally binary scheme, but one craftily re-organised so that the pivotal key of the movement turned out not to be the relative major reached at the first emphatic cadence, but the subsequent dominant minor that followed the second limb of the text, 'that the Lord God might dwell among them'. Interestingly, Handel's first version of this aria (34a/36iii/32a) made the secondary key-centres of each tonal 'half' explicit with clear instrumental interludes, but in subsequent versions he gradually covered over the internal modulatory gambit in the second half.

Like 'Thou art gone up on high', 'But who may abide' saw recomposition in different versions using the same thematic starting-point:
in its original form (5b/A2/6a) it was set as a fairly straightforward binary
movement, enlivened by some crafty delay in arriving at the central relative
major cadence. The second part of the text, 'For he is like a refiner's fire',
obviously suggested a change in musical material: in the first version the
music moves from a fearful rhetorical falling-back at the prospect of the
Messiah's arrival, to a slow roast for the 'refiner's fire', maintained within
the same overall *tempo*. When Handel re-composed the text for Guadagni
in 1750 (5/6i/6), he speeded up the 'refiner's fire' section (accompanied by
new orchestral sparks) but extended the movement with a double statement of each half of the text: four sections in all, allowing (and indeed
requiring) a more ambitious key-strategy. The first contrasted section now
moved between relative major and dominant minor, returning to the tonic
for the recapitulation statements in the second half of the aria.

Excellent as is the final version of 'But who may abide?', the arias based
on tripartite texts (such as 'Thou art gone up on high' and 'If God be for
us') show most clearly Handel's compositional skill at keeping the music 'in
the air' – maintaining and extending musical interest by arousing, fulfilling
and diverting musical expectations. The most remarkable case is 'I know
that my redeemer liveth'. This starts as if it is to be a short binary
movement (bars 1–75), possibly even the 'A' section of a *da capo* aria. But
the second layer of text, 'and tho' worms destroy this body', is followed by a
third, beginning in the subdominant at bar 119, 'For now is Christ risen'.
In the course of the movement, both the second and third parts of the text
are introduced by the opening music and text ('I know that my redeemer
liveth'), providing a unifying element through the progression of the three
biblical verses – an idea that was surely Handel's alone. At the other
extreme, 'He shall feed his flock' tickles our musical expectations in a
different way, by avoiding decisive contrasted modulations: though there
are colouristic excursions, the music returns each time to the tonic
cadence, mirroring the emotional stability of the movement's pastoral
content. It is perhaps the clearest example of a 'text-led' aria, where the
content of the words exercised close control over the formal scheme.

Choruses

In the chorus movements Handel was free of the shadow of Italian opera,
and could draw on his own considerable experience of choral writing,

developed in church music as well as in odes and oratorios. Although it is tempting to relate Handel's choral writing in some way to influences from, for example, Purcell's 'Hail, bright Cecilia' or Blow's English anthems from the period following 1697, all the elements of Handel's choral style were in evidence before he came to England, in such pieces as his D major *Laudate Pueri* and *Dixit Dominus*.

However, the balance between contrapuntal and homophonic passages was as important to the design of the choruses in *Messiah* as the employment of any choral textures and techniques previously exhibited. In responding to the biblical texts, and to Jennens's placing of the choruses within the scheme of the libretto, Handel saw opportunities for varied textural treatments within and between chorus movements, in addition to the interest provided by a number of possible tonal schemes along binary or ritornello lines. Furthermore, while arias remained principally in one 'affect' throughout (or, in exceptional cases like the Guadagni setting of 'Thou art gone up on high', two alternating 'affects'), the nature of the choruses as commentaries on the story encouraged more experimentation with appropriate contrasts of mood, speed or texture: obvious examples are found in 'Worthy is the Lamb', 'Since by man came death', the end of 'All we, like sheep', and the second text-sections of 'Surely he hath borne our griefs' and 'Behold the Lamb of God'. In only one movement, 'And with his stripes', is the music extended primarily by conventional counterpoint: more typically Handel slips easily from counterpoint to homophony as the drive of the movement seems to require, either dropping imitations in order to gather the harmonic threads at a cadential resting-point or using counterpoint (or pseudo-counterpoint) involving simultaneous long-note and short-note themes as a foil to grand chordal statements, as happens *par excellence* in the 'Hallelujah' chorus. Even in the 'Amen' chorus, contrasts of homophony–polyphony and voices–orchestra supplement the purely contrapuntal evolution of the movement. Of course Handel's contrapuntal skills, apparent in the augmentation–diminution combinations of 'Let all the Angels of God' and in the *stretti* of 'Let us break their bonds asunder'[5] as well as in the 'Amen' chorus, always serve the musico-dramatic moment.

The duet-derived choruses stand a little apart in that, by the nature of their origins, the 'contrapuntal themes' with which they begin carry their own moving-bass accompaniments. In the case of 'And he shall purify' and 'His yoke is easy', the duet-derived openings provide the themes for fully-worked contrapuntal movements with landmarked ritornello-type cadences; in 'For unto us', on the other hand, the duet-derived material deliberately retains a slender texture, acting as a foil to the full homophonic outbursts of 'Wonderful, Counsellor' with which it alternates. Except in the case of 'Lift up your heads', where the semi-chorus alternation of high and low voices required more parts on each side, Handel was content to work with four 'standard' voices throughout: it provided sufficient parts to satisfy his contrapuntal needs, however many 'real' contrapuntal lines were involved, and sufficient density for his strongest chordal gestures.

Although the choruses mainly function as discrete movements, either crowning a recitative–aria sequence or taking an independent place within the narrative or commentary, three of them are thematically integrated with the immediately preceding aria movements. As already noted, the chorus introduces the reprise of the opening music and text of 'How beautiful are the feet' in the duet-and-chorus version (36a/[38]/34). In 'O thou that tellest', the chorus provides the dramatic response to the alto soloist's call to attention in the preceding aria; Handel musically 'sets up' the chorus entry in the preceding aria by using a rondo-type form which has already seen two returns to the tonic theme before the chorus takes it up. 'But thanks be to God' begins with the theme of the preceding duet, but in the bass voice, where it provides the *background* for the chordal statement with which the chorus starts,[6] and to which the phrase 'who giveth us the victory' forms a new musical foil: the duet theme then returns to the foreground in the chorus, alternating with the new theme. While the direct thematic integration of these choruses with the preceding solo movements is of interest, however, it does not in itself betoken any exceptional emphasis on the composer's part; other choruses – indeed, all the other choruses – receive equally appropriate treatment in terms of contrast, weight and emphasis for their places in the oratorio's general scheme. Only our familiarity with the work limits our appreciation of the plasticity and variety with which Handel responded to Jennens's text.

The orchestra's contribution

The influence of trumpets and drums on some aspects of the oratorio's shape and key-scheme has already been mentioned. The string orchestra's contribution must also receive brief attention. The instrumental movements that are theirs alone, the *Sinfony* (Overture) and *Pifa* ('Pastoral Symphony'), are not mentioned in the 1743 word-book. Although printed word-books for Handel's oratorios do not normally make any reference to overtures, the silence over the *Pifa* is perhaps a little odd, and may suggest that the idea was Handel's rather than Jennens's. In context, the *Pifa* certainly provides a much-needed quiet scene-setting after the boisterousness of 'For unto us a Child is born'. The grounds for Jennens's early dissatisfaction with Handel's *Sinfony* are difficult to determine: though not unusually distinguished, it is a workmanlike piece, setting a serious tone and providing a solid tonal base of E minor, preparing and yet contrasting with the E major of the first vocal movement.

In arias and choruses the function of the orchestra was relatively conventional, doubling the voices, providing *ritornelli*, or adorning the texture with additional contrapuntal strands as appropriate. In arias, the strongest thematic commentaries from the orchestra in *Messiah* come with countermelodies or accompanying counterpoints supplied by the complete body of violins in 'unisoni' movements such as 'O thou that tellest', 'Rejoice, greatly', 'Thou art gone up on high' and 'If God be for us'. The opening ritornelli to arias and choruses generally anticipate the initial vocal theme, though usually not exactly: a precise anticipation would rob both instruments and voices of their characteristic roles. The absence of an orchestral prelude for reasons of dramatic continuity almost constitutes an effect in itself. Here again, our familiarity with the openings of 'Behold and see', 'Glory to God', 'The Lord gave the word', 'Their sound is gone out' and 'Since by man came death' may take the edge off the effect of Handel's striking vocal entry;[7] similarly we perhaps now take for granted the introduction to 'Thou shalt break them' which is 'figural' and illustrative rather than related to the singer's subsequent melodies. At the opposite extreme to the 'violini unisoni' movements come those in which Handel sets the tone of a movement or scene with a sonorous string texture, such as the opening of 'He shall feed his flock' (four parts) and the *Pifa* (three parts distributed into five by octave doublings). Within the choruses, too, the strings fill out the *tutti* texture when sonorous effects are called for, either by adding extra chordal notes above the voices (as in the final 'Amen') or by an overlay of rhythmic activity such as the lively semiquavers that decorate 'Wonderful, Counsellor'.

8

Handel's word-setting

Language, like music, communicates through sounds. It is extremely unlikely that Handel would have been insensitive to the intonations and stress patterns of the language of his adopted country in which he had lived for thirty years before composing *Messiah*. While Handel retained fluency in several languages – Italian, English, German and French – his day-to-day existence in London must have relied principally on communication in English. He may have retained traces of German inflection, but there is no reason to take seriously the caricature of Handel as a composer still acting the linguistic role of a foreigner by 1741. As with his music text, therefore, it is important to distinguish between possible 'mistakes' and positive intentions about how he wished the English to be delivered. Allowances must also be made for the possibility of changes in the conventions of pronunciation or stress during the last 250 years.

Handel certainly had some linguistic idiosyncrasies. His autograph of *Messiah* includes characteristic spellings such as 'strenght' and 'trone', and a consistent use of 'death' for 'dead'.[1] On some occasions his verbal consistency lapsed: in 'He trusted in God', for example, he wrote 'he *might* deliver him' twice, and 'he *would* deliver him' once, and he varied between 'maketh' and 'makes' in 'If God be for us'.[2] All of these might reasonably be regarded as mistakes, to be edited out with a little common sense and possibly with the arbitration of the printed libretti. But some variants – for example 'burthen' for 'burden' – have phonetic implications; and the points considered below seem to represent not mistakes but matters of deliberate aural intention. Some examples worried his contemporaries, but in many cases we can be fairly certain about Handel's attitude to suggested alternatives, and therefore about his intentions. Where such intentions are apparent, performers should surely try to follow them in the first instance, and not dismiss them as examples of linguistic incompetence.

One of the recurring idiosyncrasies of Handel's word-setting concerns his treatment of the letter 'e'. Sometimes he passes over the vowel where

Ex. 3 (a) Handel

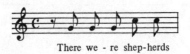

There we - re shep-herds

(b) Walsh (printed edition, *Songs in Messiah*)

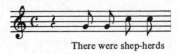

There were shep-herds

we would normally expect it to be sounded. In 'Rejoice greatly', for example, his autograph suggests that he sometimes treated 'cometh' as one syllable: this applies both to the compound-time and common-time versions.[3] More often, however, Handel separates an 'e' syllable that is normally unsounded or passed over in modern pronunciation. The treatment of 'surely' in three syllables at the beginning of 'Surely he hath borne our griefs' is not at all difficult to manage: the middle syllable may be separated (even with a rolled 'r') without distorting the word. Even some modern printed editions suppress Handel's treatment of 'were' as a disyllable at two occurrences in the nativity sequence: 'There we-re shepherds' and 'And they we-re sore afraid', yet the 1743 'But lo' (14/A6/13a) treated 'were' as a single syllable. Walsh's first editions

Ex. 4 (a) Handel

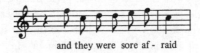

and they were sore af - raid

(b) Walsh

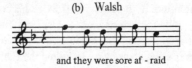

and they were sore af - raid

Ex. 5 (a)   Handel

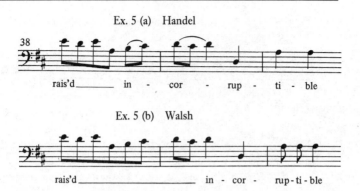

rais'd_____   in -   cor   -   rup -   ti - ble

Ex. 5 (b)   Walsh

rais'd_____   in - cor -   rup - ti - ble

'corrected' Handel's word-setting (see Ex. 3 and Ex. 4), the first example introducing a *hiatus*, and the second producing an accent on 'and'; none of the sources associated with performances by Handel and his immediate successors have any corrections at these points.[4] It is possible to deliver Handel's rhythmic intentions without laying an intrusive stress on the second syllable of 'were', and there is no reason why this should not be done.

A rather more difficult case comes with Handel's treatment of 'incorruptible' in 'The trumpet shall sound'. Here the 'problem' lies not in the number of syllables but in the stress pattern imposed by placing the second and fourth syllables on accented beats. Handel's versions and Walsh's 'solutions' are given as examples 5 and 6. Once again there are no

Ex. 6 (a)   Handel

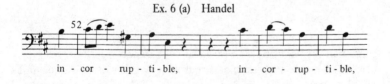

in - cor -   rup - ti - ble,   in - cor - rup - ti - ble,

Ex. 6 (b)   Walsh

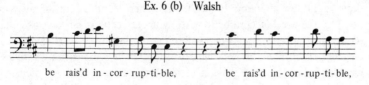

be   rais'd in - cor - rup-ti-ble,   be   rais'd in - cor -rup-ti- ble,

(and similarly at bars 91-96)

Ex. 7 (a) Handel

Come un - to__ him ' that are__ hea - vy la - den__

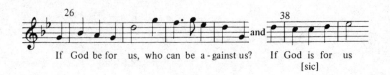

If God be for us, who can be a - gainst us? If God is for us
[sic]

Ex. 7 (b) As amended (? by Jennens) in the conducting score

Come un - to him all ye that are__ hea - vy la - den__

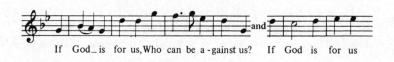

If God__ is for us, Who can be a - gainst us? If God is for us

corrections in the materials associated with Handel's performances: presumably Handel's successive bass soloists sang it as written. Although the scansion does seem rather clumsy today, bass soloists have demonstrated on modern recordings that Handel's word-setting can be sung without drawing undue attention to itself.[5] Whether Handel himself mispronounced the word (according to mid-eighteenth century conventions, that is) we shall never know. It is possible that he may have sacrificed verbal elegance at this point to rhythmic drive, assisted by some exciting percussive consonants: Walsh's version of the first passage, a longer melisma, is decidedly weak. If Handel's setting of 'incorruptible' jarred on contemporary ears, then it is surprising that Jennens did not pick him up on it, for this is just the sort of point that would have attracted his attention.

The two sets of alterations in the conducting score that appear to be in Jennens's hand both concern matters of word-setting (see Ex. 7).[6] The alteration to 'If God is/be for us' is particularly striking, not only for the word-substitution but also for the shift in the stresses and the substitution of an elegant 'sing-song' for Handel's more forceful syllabic treatment. Perhaps Jennens suggested the change after later reflection: the alterations to the word-underlay in the conducting score almost certainly date from the period between the 1743 and 1745 performances.[7] The most significant point, however, is that the alterations to 'He shall feed his flock' and 'If God be for us' in the conducting score presumably indicate improvements that Handel accepted for subsequent performances. There are no others.

This point is of some consequence with regard to 'I know that my redeemer liveth'. Jennens made elaborate amendments to the word-underlay in his personal copy of the score.[8] While we cannot be certain that his attempt to re-draft Handel's text was made during the composer's lifetime, it nevertheless seems reasonable to assume that it originated during the period of Jennens's dissatisfaction with *Messiah* in 1743–5. His alterations were so extensive that he obviously needed to try them out on his own copy before making any suggestions to Handel: the fact that no alterations were made to the conducting score indicates either that he never put the amendments forward or that Handel rejected them. The latter seems more likely, for the alterations reveal that Jennens had a completely different attitude to the treatment of the text from Handel. He introduced verbal repetitions where Handel had created long phrase-spans (though Handel did not necessarily assume that all of the long phrases would be taken in one breath); and he re-set bars 111–15 in order to remove one of the strongest features of Handel's setting – the use of 'I know that my redeemer liveth' (words and text) as the starting-point for each of the verses. But the greater part of Jennens's alterations aim to regularise the verbal stresses, so that 'stand' always takes the emphasis in 'and that he shall stand'. In doing this, Jennens seems to have completely misunderstood (or perhaps understood and been hostile to) Handel's approach to the text. Handel overlaid the lyrical character of the music with a lively variation in the stresses:

Bars 26–30 and that he shall stand at the latter day
Bars 43–7 and that he shall stand at the latter day
Bars 57–9 and that he shall stand at the latter day

Ex. 8 (a)   as first set

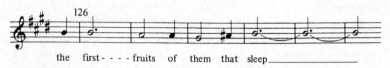

Ex. 8 (b)   as amended by Handel in composition autograph before the conducting score was copied

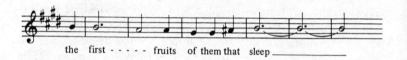

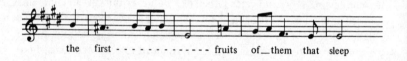

The affirmation therefore receives a different emphasis every time. This could not possibly have been the result of accident, incompetence or ignorance of English: Handel is playing with the language, and avoiding exactly that sameness that Jennens tried to impose. Walsh (or his copytext), also censored Handel's variety of emphasis: the printed editions regularised the underlay to produce predictable stress on 'he' and 'stand'. But once the sinews of Handel's word-setting have been understood, the flatness of the amended versions is soon apparent to the sensitive ear.

The care with which Handel treated this text also manifests itself towards the end, where he revised his treatment of the word 'first-fruits' during composition.[9] He first regarded it as two heavy syllables, but then altered the rhythms to lighten the second syllable, now tucked in on weak

Ex. 9 (a)   Handel (final version in composition autograph)

(* word underlay ambiguous here)

Ex. 9 (b)   as copied in the conducting score by J. C. Smith senior

beats at the end of the bar (see Ex. 8). In order to achieve this he sacrificed the word 'of', which ended up on the stressed first beat of the next bar: a slightly unfortunate verbal side-effect (which can be ameliorated in performance if the stresses of the whole phrase rather than its component bars are considered), but one that undeniably puts some impetus into the musical rhythm. There is an unsolved puzzle about the final appearance of this word in bars 150–1. Earlier in the movement, Handel arranged the stresses in this phrase to lighten the second syllable of 'first-fruits'; this placed 'of' not merely on a strong beat but on the highest and most sustained part of the phrase. For some reason Smith copied a different setting of the text into the conducting score and it was never corrected back by Handel (see Ex. 9).[10] While the conducting score version deserves some consideration, Handel's setting remains preferable: it puts a better vowel onto the top notes (allowing them to be taken smoothly into the phrase) and makes for a livelier rhythmic counterpoint with the bass at bar 150.

The word underlay in 'And with his stripes' is one of the few places in *Messiah* where Handel's intentions are unclear because he left the score to some extent unfinished.[11] Elsewhere, whether we are dealing with matters of word underlay, the combination of variant movements, or even the overall scheme of the work, we can regain Handel's view of the oratorio with considerably certainty. Such creative engagement is not a recondite and impractical undertaking. Handel did not write *Messiah* for another eighteenth-century 'interpreter': he composed, rehearsed, directed and revised the work himself, and an understanding of the oratorio requires some imaginative contact with this process. By attempting such contact we not only come nearer to the work itself, but also have a standpoint from which to judge the treatment that *Messiah* has received in the nineteenth and twentieth centuries. Of a modern staged performance of another Handel oratorio, a leading critic wrote: 'If you try to score points against Handel, you lose.'[12] With *Messiah*, which retains its riches undiminished after two and a half centuries, it is similarly more rewarding to go with the grain of Handel's score than against it.

Appendix 1: The libretto of Messiah

The following libretto gives the text as set by Handel, collated with the movement numbers used in various editions (see Preface). Another important textual source is the printed word-book for the first London performances (1743), which was almost certainly produced under the inspection of Charles Jennens and thus represents the closest source document to the libretto from which Handel originally worked in 1741. Divergences between the text of Handel's musical autograph and the 1743 libretto are collated in the notes; additions and adaptations have been made in order to cover Handel's later additions to the score. 'Scene' numberings, movement headings, capitalisation and punctuation are taken from the 1743 word-book. Handel's idiosyncratic spellings have not been noted, but his syllabic contractions (for example, 'ev'n' for 'even') have been retained: some, but not all, of these also appear in the printed libretto. (Interestingly, both Handel's autograph and the word-book distinguish between 'open'd' and 'unstopped' in 'Then shall the eyes of the blind be open'd'.)

The opening title, including the incorrect form of Handel's name and the mottoes supplied by Jennens, is taken from the title page of the 1743 word-book. The headings to Parts are those used by Handel; the word-book has the form 'Part One' (and so on). The 'Romans' text of 'How beautiful are the feet' naturally did not appear in the 1743 word-book, since it was not performed then, and for this movement reference has been made to the equivalent 1749 publication. The printed word-books set some texts in italics and some in roman type (the latter being used for recitatives), and highlight various words in the alternative type-face: the general distinction has not been repeated here, but the highlighted words are shown in italics. In his autograph, Handel headed many movements 'recit', 'accomp' and 'chorus' but put no headings for the arias, here called 'song'. In no case do his headings conflict with their equivalents in the word-book – 'RECITA-TIVE', 'RECITATIVE, accompanied' and 'CHORUS'. The headings

'SINFONY' and 'PIFA' are taken from Handel's autograph and did not appear in the word-book. 'RECITATIVE' indicates continuo-accompanied recitative, while 'RECITATIVE, accompanied' indicates recitative with orchestral accompaniment.

Voices are identified initially by the clef (*S A T B*, with no distinction between Treble and Soprano, or Alto and Contralto) in which Handel originally composed the solo part. Subsequent entries in brackets show alternative voices to which Handel at some time allocated the movement in his performances.

Abbreviations used: 'transp.' = transposed; 'var.' = variant.

Transposed versions usually entailed some modification of melodic lines in accompanying orchestral parts; in the case of 50a/52ii/– more substantial detailed recomposition was undertaken. Variants not identified as 'transpositions' are musically distinct, though some share the same thematic material.

Editorial interventions are shown in square brackets.

MESSIAH
AN
ORATORIO

Set to Musick by George-Frederic Handel, Esq;.

MAJORA CANAMUS.   *[Virgil: Eclogue IV]*

And without Controversy, great is the Mystery of Godliness: God was manifested in the Flesh, justify'd by the Spirit, seen of Angels, preached among the Gentiles, believed on in the World, received up in Glory.

In whom are hid all the Treasures of Wisdom and Knowledge.

[I Timothy 3,16; Colossians 2,3]

PART THE FIRST

Reference (B/S/T)		
0/1/1	SINFONY [Overture]	E minor

[Grave – Allegro moderato]

I

1/2/2   RECITATIVE, accompanied E major   T(S)

Comfort ye, comfort ye my People, saith your God; speak ye comfortably to *Jerusalem*, and cry unto her, that her Warfare is accomplish'd, that her Iniquity is pardon'd. The Voice of him that crieth in the Wilderness, prepare ye the Way of the Lord, make straight in the Desert a Highway for our God.

(Isaiah 40,1–3)

2/3/3   SONG   E major   T(S)   84 bars (shortened var. of 2x/–/–, 88 bars)

Ev'ry Valley shall be exalted, and ev'ry Mountain and Hill made low, the Crooked straight, and the rough Places plain.

(Isaiah 40,4)

3/4/4   CHORUS   A major

And the Glory of the Lord shall be revealed, and all Flesh shall see it together; for the Mouth of the Lord hath spoken it.

(Isaiah 40,5)

4/5/5	RECITATIVE, accompanied D minor (ending in A Major)		**B**	*HHB* Anhang (S.) gives first, unperformed, version of opening bars.

Thus saith the Lord of Hosts; Yet once a little while, and I will shake the Heav'ns and the Earth; the Sea and the dry Land: And I will shake all Nations; and the Desire of all Nations shall come. (*Haggai 2,6–7*) The Lord whom ye seek shall suddenly come to his Temple, ev'n the Messenger of the Covenant, whom ye delight in: Behold He shall come, saith the Lord of Hosts. (*Malachi 3,1*)

5/6i/6	SONG[1]	D minor	A	158 bars. *HHB* 6c

But who may abide the Day of his coming? And who shall stand when He appeareth? For He is like a Refiner's Fire. (*Malachi 3,2*)

Other settings of the same text:

5a/A5/0	Recit		B	Authenticity uncertain. *HHB* 6b
5b/A2/6a	Aria		B	136 bars; Handel's first setting. Probably never performed by Handel in this version.
5bx/–/–	Aria		B(T)	120 bars; shortened var. of 5b/A2/6a
5c/–/–	Aria	A minor	S	Transp. of 5/6i/6
–/6ii/–	Aria	G minor	S	Transp. of 5/6i/6

6/7/7	CHORUS	G minor

And He shall purify the Sons of Levi, that they may offer unto the Lord an Offering in Righteousness. (*Malachi 3,3*)

---

[1] Shown as 'RECITATIVE' in 1742, 1749 and some subsequent word-books. The recitative setting 5a/A5/6b, if authentic, may have been performed in 1742 and (less plausibly) in 1745, 1749.

II

7/8/0   RECITATIVE   A
         Behold, a Virgin shall conceive, and bear a Son, and shall call his Name *Emmanuel*, GOD WITH US.
                                                       (Isaiah 7,14; Matthew 1,23)

8/9/8   SONG   D major   A
9/9/8   CHORUS   D major   A
         O thou that tellest good Tidings to *Zion*,[2] get thee up into the high Mountain: O thou that tellest good
         Tidings to *Jerusalem*, lift up thy Voice with Strength; lift it up, be not afraid: Say unto the Cities of *Judah*,
         Behold your God. O thou that tellest good Tidings to *Zion*, Arise, shine, for thy Light is come, and the
         Glory of the Lord is risen upon thee.   *(Isaiah 40,9; Isaiah 60,1)*

10/10/9 RECITATIVE, accompanied B minor   B
         For behold, Darkness shall cover the Earth, and gross Darkness the People: but the Lord shall arise upon
         thee, and his Glory shall be seen upon thee. And the Gentiles shall come to thy Light, and Kings to the
         Brightness of thy Rising.   *(Isaiah 60,2–3)*

11/11/10 SONG   B minor   B
         The People that walked in Darkness have seen a great Light; And[3] they that dwell in the Land of the
         Shadow of Death, upon them hath the Light shined.
                                                       (Isaiah 9,2)

---

[2] Repeat of this phrase not shown in readings of 1743 printed word-book (henceforth referred to as *1743*).
[3] 'And' not included in *1743* text.

12/12/11   CHORUS   G major
For unto us a Child is born, unto us a Son is given; and the Government shall be upon his Shoulder; and His Name shall be called Wonderful, Counsellor, The Mighty God, The Everlasting Father, The Prince of Peace.
(Isaiah 9,6)

IV

13/13/12   PIFA [Pastoral symphony]   C major   32 bars; alternative 13x/13x/–, 11 bars.

14/14(a)/0   RECITATIVE   S
There were Shepherds abiding in the Field, keeping Watch over their Flock by Night.   *(Luke 2,8)*

14/14(b)/13   RECITATIVE, accompanied   F major   S   Alternative setting: Song 14a/A6/13a
[or SONG, 1743 only]
And lo, the Angel[4] of the Lord came upon them, and the Glory of the Lord shone round about them, and they were sore afraid.   *(Luke 2,9)*

14/15/0   RECITATIVE   S
And the Angel said unto them, Fear not; for behold, I bring you good Tidings of great Joy, which shall be to all People. For unto you is born this Day, in the City of *David*, a Saviour, which is Christ the Lord.
(Luke 2,10–11)

14/16/14   RECITATIVE, accompanied   D major   S
And suddenly there was with the Angel a Multitude of the heav'nly Host, praising God, and saying . . .
(Luke 2,13)

[4] The variant aria setting (14a/A6/13a) begins 'But lo, the Angel' in Handel's autograph; *1743* (heading: 'SONG') begins 'But lo, an Angel'.

15/17/15	CHORUS	D major			Glory to God in the Highest, and Peace on Earth,[5] Good Will towards Men. (*Luke 2,14*)

V

16/18/16	SONG	B flat major	S(T)	108 bars, C. *HHB* 16b	Rejoice greatly, O Daughter of *Sion*,[6] shout, O Daughter of *Jerusalem*; behold, thy King cometh unto thee: He is the righteous Saviour; and He shall speak Peace unto the Heathen. (*Zechariah 9,9–10*)

Other versions:

16a/18ii/16ax	Song	B flat major	108 bars, $\frac{12}{8}$; shortened var. of –/A7/16a.
–/A7/16a	Song	B flat major	113 bars + da capo, $\frac{12}{8}$; probably never performed by Handel in this version. S and T print this as 177 bars + *dal segno*, incorporating at the end the lead-back bars subsequently composed for 16a/18ii/16ax.

17/19i/0	RECITATIVE	S	Then shall the Eyes of the Blind be open'd, and the Ears of the Deaf unstopped; then shall the lame Man leap as a Hart, and the Tongue of the Dumb shall sing. (*Zechariah 35,5–6*)

---

5 *1743*: 'and on Earth Peace'.

6 Both Handel's autograph (henceforth *H*) and *1743* have 'Sion' here but 'Zion' elsewhere.

18/20i/17a   SONG   S

He shall feed his Flock like a shepherd: and[7] He shall gather the Lambs with his Arm, and carry them in his Bosom, and gently lead those that are with young. Come unto Him all ye that labour, come unto Him all ye that are heavy laden,[8] and He will give you Rest. Take his Yoke upon you and learn of Him; for He is meek and lowly of[9] Heart: and ye shall find Rest unto your souls.[10]

(Isaiah 40,11; Matthew 11,28–9)

Alternative Versions to 17/19i/0 and 18/20i/17a:

17/19i/0	Recitative	B flat major	S	
18/20i/17a	Song	B flat major	S	
17a/19ii/0	Recitative	F major	A	Transp. of 17/19i/0
18a/20i/17	Song	F major → B. flat major	A, then S	First half transp. from 18/20i/17a. *HHB* 17c
17b/19ii/0	Recitative	F major	A	Identical to 17a/19ii/0
18b/–/–	Song	F major	A	Transp. of 18/20i/17a. *HHB* 17b

19/21/18   CHORUS   B flat major

His Yoke is easy, his Burthen is light.[11]

(Matthew 11,30)

---

7 'and' not included in *1743* text.
8 *1743*: 'Come unto Him all ye that labour and are heavy laden'; *H*: second phrase 'Come unto him that are heavy laden', altered in conducting score (?by Jennens) to the form given here.
9 *1743*: 'lowly in Heart'.
10 *H*: 'Soul' and 'Souls' at successive occurrences.
11 *1743*: 'His Yoke is easy, and his Burden is light': Handel included 'and' only in the final phrase of the movement.

PART THE SECOND

I

20/22/19	CHORUS	G minor

Behold the Lamb of God, that taketh away the Sin of the World.[12]

(*John 1,29*)

21/23/20	SONG	E flat major A

He was despised and rejected of Men, a Man of Sorrows, and acquainted with Grief. He gave his Back to the Smiters, and his Cheeks to them that plucked off the Hair: He hid not his Face from Shame and Spitting.

(*Isaiah 53,3; Isaiah 50,6*)

22/24/21	CHORUS	F Minor

Surely he hath borne[13] our Griefs and carried our Sorrows: He was wounded for our Transgressions, He was bruised for our Iniquities; the Chastisement of our Peace was upon Him.

(*Isaiah 53,4–5*)

23/25/22	CHORUS[14]	F minor

And with His Stripes we are healed.

(*Isaiah 53,5*)

24/26/23	CHORUS	F major (ending in F minor).

All we, like Sheep, have gone astray, we have turned ev'ry one to his own Way, and the Lord hath laid on Him the Iniquity of us all.

(*Isaiah 53,6*)

---

12 *1743*: 'World!'
13 *H* and *1743*: 'born'.
14 *1743*: not shown as a separate movement, but text included in the previous chorus.

| 25/27/24 | RECITATIVE, accompanied | B flat minor (ending in E flat major) | T(S) |

All they that see him laugh him to scorn; they shoot out their Lips, and shake their Heads, saying . . . . (*Psalm 22,7*)

| 26/28/25 | CHORUS | C minor |

He trusted in God, that he would[15] deliver him: let him deliver him, if he delight in him. (*Psalm 22,8*)

| 27/29/26 | RECITATIVE, accompanied | A flat major (ending in B major) | T(S) |

Thy Rebuke hath broken his Heart; He is full of Heaviness: He looked for some to have Pity on him, but there was no Man, neither found he any to comfort him. (*Psalm 69,21*)

| 28/30/27 | SONG | E minor | T(S) |

Behold, and see, if there be any Sorrow like unto his Sorrow! (*Lamentations 1,12*)

II

| 29/31/28 | RECITATIVE, accompanied | B minor (ending in E major) | T(S) |

He was cut off out of the Land of the Living: For the Transgression of thy People was He stricken. (*Isaiah 53,8*)

[15] *H*: 'might' twice, 'would' once, altered consistently to 'would' (as *1743*) in conducting score.

30/32/29	SONG	A major	T(S)

But Thou didst not leave his Soul in Hell, nor didst Thou suffer thy Holy One to see Corruption.

(Psalm 16,10)

III

31/33/30	SEMICHORUS[16]	F major

Lift up your heads, O ye Gates, and be ye lift up, ye everlasting Doors, and the King of Glory shall come in.
Who is this King of Glory?
The Lord Strong and Mighty; the Lord Mighty in Battle.
Lift up your Heads, O ye Gates, and be ye lift up, ye everlasting Doors, and the King of Glory shall come in.
Who is this King of Glory? The Lord of Hosts: he is the King of Glory.

(Psalm 24,7–10)

IV

32/34/0	RECITATIVE	T(S)

Unto which of the Angels said He at any time, Thou art my Son, this Day have I begotten thee?

(Hebrews 1,5)

33/35/31	CHORUS	D major

Let all the Angels of God worship Him.

(Hebrews 1,6)

[16] *1743* repeats 'SEMICHORUS' headings above each of the five sections of text, though Handel set the final section for full voices. Handel's heading for the movement was simply 'Corus'.

V

34/36i/32	SONG[17]	D minor	A	*HHB* 32b

Thou art gone up on High; Thou hast led Captivity captive, and received Gifts for Men, yea, even for thine Enemies, that the Lord God might dwell among them. *(Psalm 68:18)*

Other settings of the same text:

34a/36iii/32a	Song	D minor	B	Handel's first setting
34b/A10/32b	Song	D minor	S	*HHB* 32c[18]
34c/36ii/–	Song	G minor	S	Transp. of 34/36i/32. *HHB* 32d

35/37/33	CHORUS	B flat major

The Lord gave the Word: Great was the Company of the Preachers. *(Psalm 68,11)*

Alternative sequence I, with Romans text for 36/38/34

36/38i/34ax	SONG [1745 onwards]	G minor	S	24 bars: shortened var. of –/A13/34a. *HHB* 34c

How beautiful are the Feet of them that preach the Gospel of Peace, and bring glad Tidings of good Things. *(Romans 10,15)*

---

[17] 1742, 1749 and subsequent word-books head this, probably erroneously, as 'RECITATIVE'.
[18] *HHB* gives voice as 'Alto', but Handel wrote the movement in the Soprano clef, and all editions designate it for Soprano.

−/A13/34a	Song	G minor		S	35 bars + *da capo*. Probably never performed by Handel in this form.
36b/38ii/34b	Song	C minor	A		*HHB* 34d.
37/39/35a	CHORUS [1745 onwards][19]	E flat major			Text previously included in −/13A/34a. *HHB* 35b.

Their Sound is gone out into all Lands, and their Words unto the Ends of the World. (*Romans 10,18*)

Alternative sequence II, with Isaiah text for 36/38/34

36a/[38]/34	DUETTO and CHORUS [1742–3]	D minor	AA		*HHB* 34b

How beautiful are the feet of him that bringeth glad Tidings,[20] Tidings of Salvation; that saith[21] unto Sion, thy God reigneth.[22] Break forth into Joy, glad Tidings, thy God reigneth. (*Isaiah 52,7–9*)

Another version:

36ax/[38x]/−	Duetto and Chorus			SA	Solo parts adapted from preceding version, remainder identical
37a/39ii/35	SONG [1743 only][23]	F major		T(S)	Also printed S A14. *HHB* 35a.

Their Sound is gone out into all Lands, and their Words unto the Ends of the World. (*Romans 10,18*)

---

19 *H*: text originally set as central section of preceding aria (−/13A/34a), but never performed thus.
20 *H*: 'How beautiful are the Feet of them that bring good Tidings.'   21 *1743*: 'say'.
22 *1743* does not distinguish chorus text, concluding: 'thy God reigneth, break forth into Joy, thy God reigneth!'   23 See n. 19.

VI

38/40ii/36x	SONG	C major	B	45 bars, partly derived from 38a/40i/36. *HHB* 36b

Why do the Nations so furiously rage together? and why do the People imagine a vain Thing? The Kings of the Earth rise up, and the Rulers take Counsel[24] together against the Lord and against his Anointed.
(*Psalm 2,1–2*)

Alternative version:

38a/40i/36	Song	C major		96 bars. *HHB* 36a. Probably never performed by Handel in this form.
39/41/37	CHORUS	C major		(*Psalm 2,3*)

Let us break their Bonds asunder, and cast away their Yokes from us.

VII

40/42/0	RECITATIVE		T	He that dwelleth in Heaven shall laugh them to scorn; the Lord shall have them in Derision. (*Psalm 2,4*)
41/43/38	SONG	A minor	T	*HHB* 38a

Thou shalt break them with a Rod of Iron; thou shalt dash them in[25] pieces like a Potter's Vessel.
(*Psalm 2,9*)

Alternative setting (texts of 40/42/0 and 41/43/38 as one movement):

41a/A14/0	Recitative		T(S)	B prints with 40 as '40a/41a'. *HHB* 38b

[24] *H*: 'Counsel' once, 'Counsels' twice in first setting; 'Counsels' in 38a/40i/36.

[25] *H*: 'to' at one occurrence, 'in' elsewhere.

42/44/39 CHORUS D major

Hallelujah! for the Lord God Omnipotent reigneth. The Kingdom of this World is become the Kingdom of our Lord and of his Christ; and He shall reign for ever and ever, King of Kings, and Lord of Lords. Hallelujah!

(Revelation 19,6; 11,15; 19,16)

PART THE THIRD

I

43/45/40 SONG E major **S**

I know that my Redeemer liveth, and that He shall stand at the latter Day upon the Earth: And tho' Worms destroy this Body, yet in my Flesh shall I see God. For now is Christ risen from the Dead, the First-Fruits of them that sleep.

(Job 19, 25–6; 1 Corinthians 15,20)

44/46/41 CHORUS A minor

Since by Man came Death, by Man came also the Resurrection of the Dead.[26] For as in *Adam* all die, even so in *Christ* shall all be made alive.

(1 Corinthians 15,21–2)

II

45/47/42 RECITATIVE, accompanied D major **B**

Behold, I tell you a Mystery: We shall not all sleep, but we shall all be chang'd, in a Moment, in the Twinkling of an Eye, at the last Trumpet. *(1 Corinthians 15,51–2)*

---

[26] *H*: 'Death'.

46/48/43	SONG	D major	B	213 bars + *dal segno*: amended from –/48x/–. *HHB* 43b

The Trumpet shall sound, and the Dead[27] shall be rais'd incorruptible, and We shall be chang'd. For this corruptible must put on Incorruption, and this Mortal must put on Immortality. (*1 Corinthians 15,52–4*)

Alternative version:

–/48x/–	Song			213 bars + *da capo*. *HHB* 43a. Probably never performed by Handel in this form.

III

47/49/0	RECITATIVE		A

Then shall be brought to pass the Saying that is written; Death is swallow'd up in Victory. (*1 Corinthians 15,54*)

48/50/44x	DUETTO	E flat major	AT	24 bars, shortened from –/A15/44. *HHB* 44b

O Death, where is thy Sting? O Grave, where is thy Victory? The Sting of Death is Sin, and the Strength of Sin is the Law. (*1 Corinthians 15,55–6*)

Other settings of the same text:

–/A15/44	Duetto			41 bars. *HHB* 44a. Probably never performed Handel in this form.
–/A16/–	Recitative		A, then A	Authenticity doubtful

[27] *H*: 'Death'.

49/51/45	CHORUS	E flat major	

CHORUS (49/51/45) — E flat major
But Thanks be to God, who giveth Us the Victory through our Lord Jesus Christ.   *(1 Corinthians 15,57)*

SONG (50/52a/46) — G minor — S — Opening text changed at early date. *HHB 46a*
If God be for us,[28] who can be against us? Who shall lay anything to the Charge of God's Elect? It is God that justifieth; Who is he that condemneth? It is Christ that died, yea, rather that is risen again; who is at the Right Hand of God, who maketh[29] intercession for us.   *(Romans 8,31 and 33–4)*

Alternative version:

Song (50a/52ii/–) — C minor — A — Transp. of 50/52i/46, with recomposition

IV

CHORUS (51/53/47) — D major
Worthy is the Lamb that was slain, and hath redeemed us to God by His Blood, to receive Power, and Riches, and Wisdom, and Strength, and Honour, and Glory, and Bleasing. Blessing and Honour, Glory and Pow'r[30] be unto Him that sitteth upon the Throne, and unto the Lamb, for ever and ever.   *(Revelation 5,12–14)*

Alternative version:

Chorus (51x/53x/–) — 51/53/47 with 14-bar cut

CHORUS (52/53/47) — *HHB 48*
Amen

---

28 This is Handel's original form (as also *1743*, and *1749* word-book), later altered to 'If God is for us' in the conducting score (as *1742* word-book).
29 *H*: 'makes' four times (two in a passage later cancelled) and 'maketh' twice.
30 *H*: 'Blessing, and Honour, and Glory, and Power'.

The early word-books

Although it is impossible to recover any changes or omissions that Handel may have made to the libretto during the course of composition, comparison between the 1742 Dublin and 1743 London word-books is useful in view of Jennens's adverse reaction to the former. The 1743 word-book is certainly more elegantly laid out and punctuated, but Jennens over-reacted when he described the Dublin word-book as 'full of Bulls'.[31] His hostility may have been aroused by a mistake in the text of the very first vocal movement: in 'Comfort ye' the word 'God' is twice replaced by 'Lord'. On the next page, in 'Thus saith the Lord', the text 'And I will shake all nations' is inverted to 'all Nations I will shake'. Thereafter, however, mistakes of this type are relatively few. They may have occurred because Handel supplied George Faulkner, the Dublin printer, with a new copy-text – perhaps written out partly from memory – and not with a simple copy of Jennens's original. The complete text of 'He shall feed his flock/Come unto him' in the 1742 word-book is almost precisely that set by Handel, even down to word repetitions, but it was substantially amended for the 1743 word-book: the issue of what Handel performed is complicated by the fact that Jennens himself may have intervened in 1743 to alter the word-setting in the conducting score.[32]

More seriously, the 1742 word-book originally omitted the recitative 'Unto which of the Angels', which had to be re-inserted with a paste-over slip.[33] However, the attendant confusion at this point probably resulted in an incorrect heading 'Recitative' above 'Thou art gone up on high'. Jennens may have regarded the omission of 'Their sound is gone out' from the Dublin word-book as another printer's error: but Handel's Dublin re-setting of 'How beautiful are the Feet' had eliminated this text, and the word-book accurately reflected what was performed. In 1743 Jennens changed the layout of 'Lift up your heads' into a 'question-and-answer' format (with 'Semi-chorus' headings) that was obviously appropriate to Handel's setting.[34] On the other hand, he eliminated from the 1743 word-book the 'Da Capo' directions from Dublin that usefully signalled the

---

[31] Letter of 21 February 1742/3, quoted in chapter 3, pp. 24–5.
[32] See chapter 8, p. 79 and Ex. 7.
[33] See Burrows, 'The Autographs', where this is illustrated.
[34] In doing so he may have been restoring the textual layout to the one that Handel had originally received and responded to.

reputation of texts. But in general the changes in the 1743 word-book bring the printed text closer to that set by Handel.[35]

The text of the 1749 word-book is something of a curiosity; it appears to have been set up, not from Jennens's 1743 text, but from a half-corrected copy of the Dublin 1742 word-book. In many details the 1749 text retains errors from 1742, and the probably erroneous heading 'Recitative' for 'Thou art gone up on high' must surely have been derived from the same source. It is uncertain which version of that movement was performed in 1749, though the soprano version composed for 1743 (34b/A10/32b) seems most likely.[36]

---

[35] In the following phrases, however, the 1742 word-book is more faithful than that of 1743 to Handel's text: 'And lo, the Angel of the Lord', 'He is meek and lowly of heart', 'His burthen is light', 'How beautiful are the feet of him', 'For now is Christ risen from the death', 'The resurrection of the death', 'and the death shall be raised'.

[36] The negative evidence supporting this is that none of the primary sources for the other versions bear the ripieno markings which Handel added throughout the conducting score in 1749: it seems reasonable to suppose that such markings might have been added to the performance copy of 34b/A10/32b, which is now lost.

Appendix 2: Messiah sources

The history of the development of *Messiah* from initial composition to Handel's last active performances has to be reconstructed from an interpretation of surviving materials of various sorts, such as musical manuscripts, printed libretti, letters and newspaper reports. The outline offered presents the author's conclusions, with only passing references to the complex interaction of information from the sources that lie behind them.[1] However, it is impossible to frame any coherent history of the development of Handel's *Messiah* without some reference to the most important sources.

The composition autograph

This manuscript[2] contains principally the autograph score composed, according to the dates that Handel himself added, between 22 August and 14 September 1741. Of the preliminary sketching process that may have preceded this autograph, only a single page survives (now in the collection of Handel's manuscript material at the Fitzwilliam Museum, Cambridge):[3] it comprises jottings for the 'Amen' chorus, 'He was despised' and 'Let all the angels of God', the latter with an alternative text suggesting that Handel considered trying the same theme for 'and cast away their yokes from us' in 'Let us break their bonds'. Although other works from which Handel drew music – such as the Italian Duets – may be regarded as sources for *Messiah*, they cannot be regarded as composition sketches.

Handel's autograph contains amendments obviously made during com-

---

[1] The foundation studies for modern interpretations of the source history are Larsen, *Handel's 'Messiah'*, and Shaw, *A Textual and Historical Companion*. These have been further refined by Burrows, 'Handel's Performances' and 'The Autographs'.

[2] British Library RM 20.f.2. For a full description of this and other *Messiah* sources, see the items cited in note 1.

[3] Cambridge, Fitzwilliam Museum, Mu.MS 263 p. 58. This page, and some independent canonic exercises on the subject of the 'Amen' fugue (now in Cfm Mu.MS 260), are reproduced with Chrysander's facsimile of *Messiah*. See Gudger, 'Sketches and Drafts'.

position, others that antedate the first performances, and singers' names and annotations added by Handel after his return from Dublin, in preparation for the first London performances in 1743. Although Handel himself ceased to work from his autograph for any practical purpose after 1743, it was later used by scribes as a copy-text for some manuscripts, and also became a useful filing centre for autographs of additional movements composed during 1742–5, which were included with the main autograph when it was first securely bound, probably in the 1790s.[4]

The conducting score

The term 'conducting score' is now generally accepted for the fair-copy scores made for Handel soon after he completed the autographs of his major works, and put to practical use by him in performances. While it is not entirely certain that the conducting score of *Messiah*[5] regularly stood on the music desk of Handel's harpsichord, from which he no doubt conducted performances of *Messiah*, it was nevertheless used by him in the preparation of his performances, and contains many additions and annotations in his hand. It was copied by J. C. Smith senior, almost certainly in September–October 1741 before Handel left London for Dublin, and while the composer himself was at work on the first draft of *Samson*.

The conducting score saw various structural changes, even during Handel's lifetime: unnecessary material was, wherever possible, ejected whenever it fell decisively out of use, and new music (some in the composer's hand) was inserted as it entered the scheme of Handel's performances. The score carries several layers of singers' names and transposition directions, entered by Handel and his immediate successors, presumably as guides to music copyists as they prepared the performing materials. In addition, the conducting score carries some detailed musical revisions in Handel's hand, including the orchestral 'ripieno' directions added in 1749 (see chapter 4).

---

4 Prior to receiving their 'Royal Library' bindings, Handel's autographs were probably kept as loose fascicles, possibly lightly secured with threads. See Burrows and Ronish, *A Catalogue*, introduction.
5 Oxford, Bodleian Library MSS Tenbury 346,347; three volumes, now bound as two. See, in addition to the references cited in note 1, Shaw, *Handel's Conducting Score*, and Clausen, *Händels Direktionspartituren.* Unqualified references to 'conducting score' in this book refer to the 'Tenbury' score: a second conducting score, now at Hamburg, was prepared in Handel's last years.

The Foundling Hospital material

In the third codicil to Handel's will, dated 30 July 1757, he bequeathed 'a fair copy of the Score and all Parts of my Oratorio called The Messiah to the Foundling Hospital'.[6] This material was copied in 1759 and remains today in the collection of the Hospital's successor, the Thomas Coram Foundation. It now consists of a three-volume score and twenty-eight part-books (thirteen vocal and fifteen orchestral) copied by three scribes – Smith senior, S5 and S6:[7] it lacks the part-book for the principal soprano soloist, but it is not known whether this was accidentally omitted in 1759 or whether it has been lost. Principal interest attaches to the part-books, which seem to have been copied from another set of parts that originated in 1754. The set includes oboe and bassoon parts derived by the copyists, presumably to Handel's directions, from the appropriate lines of the score: in this all-important matter the part-books show not only which movements should include those instruments, but also the extent to which their parts should double the violin, treble voice or basso continuo lines. Complementing the part-books are lists of performers for *Messiah* in the Foundling Hospital accounts from 1754, 1758, 1759 and beyond.[8]

Printed word-books

The publication of printed texts for Handel's London oratorios was a continuation from established operatic practice. The word-books (libretti) were sold at the theatres, and sometimes also at the offices of the printer–publisher, on the days of performances and perhaps also during the few days preceding. Printed *Messiah* word-books survive for Handel's performances in 1742, 1743, 1749, 1750, 1755, 1758 and 1759, along with a number of undated issues that were probably connected with Handel's performances in the unaccounted-for years of the 1750s.[9] It is also possible that remaining old stock was re-sold for performances in years subsequent to those named on the title pages. Printed libretti need to be approached with some critical caution: in the nature of the case, they were often put together rather hurriedly.

---

[6] Deutsch, *Handel*, p. 509.
[7] 'S5' and similar references to copyists throughout this book are based on the designations in Larsen, *Handel's 'Messiah'*.
[8] Reprinted Deutsch, *Handel*, pp. 751, 800–1, 825.
[9] See Shaw, *A First List*; since that publication, a copy of the 1743 word-book has been discovered. None of the word-books from Handel's life-time mention the Foundling Hospital on their title pages.

Early musical copies, manuscript and printed

Some eighteenth-century manuscripts preserve music that has not survived in the composition autograph or Handel's conducting score. The 'Granville' copy of *Messiah*[10] (copied *c*.1743–4), for example, includes 34b/A10/32b and 50a/52ii/–: the first of these movements also appears in a very early manuscript copy recently added to the Coke Collection.[11] The 'Matthews' copy,[12] prepared by John Matthews between 1761 and 1765 from musical sources then found in Salisbury, Winchester and Durham, includes 18b/–/– and the possibly authentic 5a/A5/0. Matthews also incorporated into his score the oboe parts and the vocal ornamentation to some of the arias that he found in his sources: although neither of these features derived directly from Handel's performances, they give an insight into contemporary performance practices. Eighteenth-century vocal ornamentation is also found in the 'Goldschmidt' score,[13] a manuscript copied by S1 and S5 which originated in about 1743–5 and was owned by William Hayes.[14]

The *Messiah* materials associated with the librettist Charles Jennens are of particular interest. He owned a three-volume manuscript score,[15] a set of performing parts copied directly from Handel's autograph and textually independent of his score,[16] and 'top-up' copies of versions of movements composed after his score was copied.[17] There is also an uncompleted keyboard arrangement of the first half of Part One in his hand that for some mysterious reason found its way into the Royal Music Library along with Handel's autographs.[18] Rather surprisingly, these manuscripts throw little light on the librettist's relationship with the composer: the most significant feature from this point of view is Jennens's attempt to re-write the word-underlay of 'I know that my Redeemer liveth'.

Many eighteenth-century manuscript scores are not copies taken

---

[10] British Library Egerton MS 2937.
[11] See Burrows, 'Newly-recovered "Messiah" Scores'.
[12] Dublin, Archbishop Marsh's Library, St Patrick's Cathedral, Z 1.2.26.
[13] New York, Pierpont Morgan Library, Cary MS 122.
[14] It is possible that some of the ornamentation is in Hayes's hand: if it relates to Hayes's own performance it is of particular interest since some of the soloists he employed had also sung for Handel.
[15] Manchester Public Libraries, Newman Flower Collection, Henry Watson Music Library, MS 130 Hd4 vols. 198–200.
[16] Manchester Public Libraries in MS 130 Hd4 vols. 142–9, 247–8, 353.
[17] British Library, in RM 19.a.2.
[18] British Library, RM 19.d.1.

directly from the autograph or conducting score, but are copies of copies; the early printed editions have a similarly distant status. John Walsh's first publications of the arias from *Messiah*[19] were derived from a copy-text that originated before 1745, even though many of the publications themselves did not appear until much later. The copy-text included several variants specific to Handel's 1743 performances, which therefore received an emphasis in print that bore no relation to Handel's own practice.[20] Walsh's copy-text contained versions that Handel probably never performed of 'Rejoice, greatly' and 'Why do the nations'.

The plates of Walsh's *Songs in Messiah* were re-used, in conjunction with new plates for the choruses and other material, in the first printed full score of 1767. The title, *Messiah An Oratorio in Score As it was Originally Perform'd. Compos'd by Mr. Handel To which are added His additional Alterations*, was misleading, but the main text and appendix together provided a compendious selection of variant movements.[21] The *Messiah* score in Arnold's edition (1787–8) also contains some variant movements.[22] While the eighteenth-century printed publications deserve the same critical attention as other secondary manuscript sources for *Messiah*, it would obviously be ridiculous to invest their contents with the sort of authority that attaches to the autograph and conducting score.[23]

Facsimiles

Handel's composition autograph and his conducting score have both been reproduced in their entirety. The autograph has been published twice, in London by the Sacred Harmonic Society in 1868 and in Hamburg for the Händelgesellschaft in 1892; the latter, which includes an introduction by Friedrich Chrysander, was reprinted by the Da Capo Press (New York) in 1969. A facsimile of the conducting score was published by The Scolar Press, London, for the Royal Musical Association in 1974.

Musical facsimiles from composers' autographs are inherently attractive and give the reader a sense of moving closer to the creative process, but

[19] See Shaw, *A Textual and Historical Companion*, chapter 6; Smith, *Handel*, p. 116ff.; and Burrows, 'Handel and the Foundling Hospital', pp. 279–80.

[20] This also applies to many early manuscript copies: see Burrows, 'The Autographs'.

[21] There seems to be a close relationship between the contents of this score and an earlier manuscript copy, Cambridge, Fitzwilliam Museum, Mu.MS 844 (The 'Lennard' copy).

[22] See Smith, *Handel*, p. 129. Arnold cast around for all the *Messiah* movements he could find; there seems to be no direct relationship between his edition and the manuscript score that he owned, now Glasgow University Library, Euing Music Collection R.d.20.

[23] See Shaw, *A Textual and Historical Companion*, chapter 7.

their apparent authority can be deceptive; the performance history of *Messiah* is complex and it is easy to draw the wrong conclusions. Sometimes a textual issue turns not on the present appearance of a source, but on what it may have looked like at a certain date. The sources therefore need interpretation, and the considered conclusions of a modern editor may be more reliable than the appearance of Handel's intentions in his scores.

Notes

1 The historical background

1 See Zachow (Zachau), Friedrich Wilhelm, *Gesammelte Werke*, ed. Seiffert, revised Moser, *Denkmäler deutscher Tonkunst* XXI, XXII, re-issued in one volume (Wiesbaden 1958). For a broader survey of German church music in Handel's youth, see Bernd Baselt, 'Handel and his Central German Background' in Sadie and Hicks, *Handel Tercentenary Collection*, p. 43.

2 The tension between dramatic musical realism and religious decorum is, however, revealed in the preface to Heinrich Schütz's *Auferstehungs-Historie* (Resurrection Oratorio) of 1623: Schütz gave the narrating evangelist to a solo voice, but the words of Christ are set for alto and tenor duet.

3 Bach himself copied part of a score of Handel's *Brockes Pasion*.

4 See Graydon Beeks, 'Handel and Music for the Earl of Carnarvon' in *Bach, Handel, Scarlatti: Tercentenary Essays*, ed. Peter Williams (Cambridge 1985), pp. 16–18.

5 The autograph page that would have carried the title is missing, but this title appears on the authoritative manuscript copy from the Malmesbury Collection.

6 Burney, *An Account*, 'Fifth Performance', pp. 100–1.

7 Though a contemporary pamphlet complained that two of the Italian singers 'made rare work with the *English* Tongue you would have sworn it had been *Welch*' (*See and Seem Blind*, p. 16; Deutsch, *Handel*, p. 301).

8 See Carole Taylor, 'Handel's Disengagement from Italian Opera' in Sadie and Hicks, *Handel Tercentenary Collection*, p. 165.

2 From composition to first performance

1 The draft score in its final form comprised 130 ten-stave folios: this figure does not include any folios discarded during composition, or the part-folio carrying Handel's early revision to the Pifa. In the six days following 22 August he drafted fifty folios (100 page-sides) for Part One, more than eight per day.

2 'Filled-up' ('ausgefüllet') was Handel's own phrase; I have borrowed 'framing' from Sullivan.

3 This may be inferred from the fact that Jennens never held the office of magistrate which would have been conventional for someone of his social standing.

4 He inherited the estate outright in 1747.

5 See Ruth Smith, 'The Achievements', for a major study of Jennens.

6 In one of the first surviving letters (11 July 1731) Holdsworth concludes his decription of an opera in Naples with 'the finest voices in the world signify nothing without a H----l'.

7 Quotations from letters (which retain original spellings and punctuation) begin with a literal transcription of place and date. Correspondents are identified as GFH (Handel), CJ (Jennens) and EH (Holdsworth). I thank Gerald Coke for granting permission before his death for quotation from unpublished sections of the Jennens–Holdsworth letters. Some extracts from the correspondence are included in Eisen and Eisen *Händel-Handbuch*, 4; all quotations in the present book have been checked against the originals.

8 Jennens's incomplete keyboard MS of *Messiah* is now British Library RM 19.d.1; his music collection, including scores bearing additional figurings in Jennens's hand, was bequeathed to the Earls of Aylesford and the greater part of this 'Aylesford Collection' is now in the Henry Watson Music Library, Manchester Central Libraries.

9 British Library RM 20.g.3 and RM 20.d.10.

10 On *Saul*, see Hicks, 'Handel, Jennens and "Saul"'; for *Belshazzar*, the pre-composition contacts are recorded in a series of letters from Handel to Jennens (Deutsch, *Handel*, pp. 592–6).

11 In spite of his partisanship in favour of Handel, Jennens apparently expected to have some influence on the musical programme of the new opera company: in the same letter of 10 July he encouraged Holdsworth to obtain manuscript copies of operas by Latilla and Jommelli so that 'if they deserve it we may have them perform'd on the English Stage'.

12 Handel may possibly have made a trip to Gopsal during May–June, but there is no evidence for this and Jennens was sensitive about receiving visitors there because he felt that he could not entertain them properly (letter CJ to EH 24 July 1736). Handel was certainly in London in July, for he gave the place and date of composition on the autographs of the Italian duets that he composed on 1 and 3 July (now in British Library RM 20.g.9).

13 It is not certain whether by 'Passion Week' Jennens meant the week before Easter (referred to as 'Holy Week' in the Book of Common Prayer) or the preceding week, which commences with Passion Sunday. In his letter Jennens may also have been recalling Handel's benefit *Oratorio* of 28 March 1738, which fell within Holy Week.

14 Handel did not date the beginning of *Samson*: he completed the draft of Part One on 29 September (RM 20.f.6 f.54v).

15 The two principal compositional 'layers' of RM 20.f.6 can be distinguished, and the main outlines of the draft of 1741 undoubtedly included these instruments. The inclusion of trombones is particularly suggestive: these were only available in London, and only for a limited period: see Donald Burrows, 'Handel, the Dead March and a Newly-identified Trombone Movement', *Early Music*, 18 (1990), p. 408.

16 William Boyce composed or adapted music for Dublin performances at this period, though he never went there himself: see Ian Bartlett and Robert J. Bruce 'William Boyce's "Solomon"', *Music & Letters*, 61 (1980), p. 28.

17 *The Dublin Journal*, 21 November 1741; Deutsch, *Handel*, p. 525.

18 Handel's letter to Jennens of 29 December 1741 (quoted pp. 15–16) suggests that the Lord Lieutenant (William Cavendish, Third Duke of Devonshire) actively supported his performances and, further, that King George II's assent to Handel's absence from London was required.

19 The first performance of *Judas Maccabaeus* (1 April 1747) may possibly have been undertaken by such a four-voice cast, though it seems probable that a second soprano was added either before or during the first run of performances: five soloists would certainly have been needed for the performances of *Joseph* that immediately preceded *Judas Maccabaeus*.

20 See Boydell, *A Dublin Musical Calendar*, pp. 262, 268.

21 Boydell, *ibid.*, p. 272. As in London, the leading cathedral singers held offices in two or more choirs simultaneously.

22 Bailey and Mason are mentioned on the conducting score of *L'Allegro*, but the identity of the leading male soloists for most of Handel's programme remains a little vague, apart from the tenor Calloghan, who held no cathedral appointment.

23 See Deutsch, *Handel*, pp. 536–7. The result of Swift's appeal to the Cathedral Chapter is apparently not known.

24 For full text, see Deutsch, *Handel*, p. 538.

25 This collaboration may be inferred from the ticket arrangements: for his own subscription series, tickets had been sold from Handel's house. For the second *Messiah* performance, tickets were sold through both agencies.

26 Deutsch, *Handel*, p. 541. Since it seems that some part of the profits from all performances in the Hall went to the Charitable Musical Society (see note 20 above), a defence of the performances on account of their general charitable objects might have already been made a few weeks before, in response to Dean Swift's memorandum.

27 *The Dublin Journal*, 10–13 April 1742; the transcription in Eisen and Eisen, *Händel-Handbuch*, 4, p. 348 is more accurate than that in Deutsch, *Handel*, p. 545.

28 If this were not a charity performance, the choirs from the two cathedrals might not have been allowed to perform. Such a situation would have entailed considerable re-arrangement of the score, which Handel had adapted to the conditions of the first performance. But perhaps, having agreed once to the use of their singers, the Deans and Chapters were inclined to fight no more.

29 The work's ready acceptance in Dublin is confirmed by the fact that it subsequently received annual performances there throughout Handel's lifetime, even during years when Handel himself did not produce the oratorio in London: see Boydell, *A Dublin Musical Calendar*.

30 Deutsch, *Handel*, pp. 546–7.

31 Copy, in the hand of J. C. Smith senior, now in the Coke Handel Collection: Handel enclosed this with his letter to Jennens of 9 September 1742. The full text is printed in Eisen and Eisen, *Händel-Handbuch*, 4, pp. 353–4.

32 Mainwaring *Memoirs*, p. 131; Burney, *An Account*, 'Sketch of the Life of Handel', p. 25.

33 Burney, *ibid.*, p. 26. See Charles Cudworth, 'Mythistorica Handeliana' in *Festskrift Jens Peter Larsen* (Copenhagen 1972). Burney does not say that he witnessed the incident himself.

34 The manuscript paper of the *Messiah* conducting score is of the same type as some that Handel used in the autograph of *Samson*. Smith senior and S4 copied insertions in the conducting scores relating to revisions that Handel made to his works for Dublin performances.

35 Victor Schoelcher, *The Life of Handel* (London 1857), p. 249, quoting 'Fragmenta' from 'The library of the British Museum'.

36 The airs, mostly by Handel, that Mrs Cibber sang at her independent performances in London during the 1730s were taken predominantly from soprano roles: it may be that, in undertaking Handel's alto-clef music in 1741–4, she departed from her most natural register and had to compensate with dramatic 'presence'.

37 Thomas Sheridan, *British Education* (1756), quoted in Robert Manson Myers, *Handel's Messiah: A Touchstone of Taste* (New York 1948), p. 100.

38 Burney, *An Account*, 'Sketch of the Life of Handel', p. 27.

39 Another, more straightforward, alto transposition may have been used in the 1750s: see Burrows, 'The Autographs', p. 216.

40 The recitative is found in the Matthews' manuscript and Arnold's printed edition. See note 1 to the libretto (p. 87) and Burrows, 'The Autographs', pp. 210–21.

41 British Library K.8.d.4. See Shaw, *A Textual and Historical Companion*, pp. 109–111.

42 Deutsch, *Handel*, pp. 524–5, p. 551.

3 The first London performances

1 Deutsch, *Handel*, p. 553.

2 Eisen and Eisen, *Händel-Handbuch*, 4, p. 355.

3 It is not known whether there had been any further contact between Handel and Jennens; it may be significant that Jennens had advance information about *Samson*.

4 See the entry for 15 March 1743 in Deutsch, *Handel*, p. 562.

5 The reading of 'B^{ps}' is itself uncertain in the original.

6 See, for example, Holdsworth's letter of 15 March 1737, quoted in chapter 2, p. 15.

7 See, for example, Charles Wesley's comment on J. F. Lampe in his Journal for 7 October 1749, quoted in [Handel], *The Complete Hymns and Chorales*, facsimile edition with introduction by Donald Burrows (London, 1988), p. 3.

8 Deutsch, *Handel*, pp. 854–5: letter of 25 May 1780. Compare John Hawkins's description of Handel in his last years attaining a 'solid and rational piety', and displaying 'the utmost fervour of devotion' at services at St George's Church, Hanover Square, in *A General History of the Science and Practice of Music* (London 1776), Book 20 (1853/1968 edn in 2 vols., London/New York, 2, p. 910).

9 *The Dublin Journal* reported the Royal Family's attendance at the fourth night of *Samson* in 1743 (see note 4, *supra*), with no specific mention of the King. The next reported Royal visit to an oratorio was by Princess Amelia in March 1750 (to *Theodora*): ten years later she became the first member of the family with a recorded attendance at *Messiah*, at the Foundling Hospital.

10 Lord Hay's son was born in London on 12 August 1742, and it may be assumed that he was there for the 1742–3 season. See the entry for Thomas, Ninth Earl of Kinnoull in James Balfour Paul (ed.), *The Scots Peerage founded on Wood's Edition of Sir Robert Douglas's Peerage of Scotland*, vol. 5 (Edinburgh 1908), p. 234.

11 Probably written in 1760. Deutsch, *Handel*, p. 848.

12 A photographic reproduction of this copy is available in the Gerald Coke Collection; the present author examined the original in 1984.

13 Deutsch, *Handel*, p. 560.

14 Beard and Miss Edwards had also performed in the Drury Lane company for the 1740–1 season.

15 Burney, *A General History of Music*, Book 4 (London 1789), chapter 12 (in 2 vols., New York 1935/1957, vol. 2, p. 1010). The description is confirmed by Handel's actions in 1743 when it seems probable that Beard fell out of the cast towards the end of the season: Beard's role in *Samson* was drastically cut for Lowe, and most of Beard's music in *Messiah* went to Avolio.

16 It seems that Handel in 1743 had not yet evolved smooth practical arrangements for dealing with performing material for the oratorios, as he began to note the re-distribution of the solo music on his composition autographs of *Messiah* and *Samson*, instead of on the conducting scores that normally served as his 'master copies'. He had worked half way through *Messiah* before he turned his attention to the conducting score.

17 The autograph of this movement is lost: the earliest sources are in the 'Granville' manuscript and a recently acquired copy in the Coke Collection.

18 The 'Matthews' manuscript and Arnold's edition: see Burrows, 'The Autographs', pp. 210–11.

19 From Handel's markings on the autograph and conducting score: see Burrows, 'Handel's Performances', further amended by 'The Autographs'.

20 See Burrows, 'Handel's Performances'.

21 Miss Edwards was also in Handel's company at the time and should have been available if another soprano was required. However, there is considerable doubt as to whether Miss Edwards sang in *Messiah*: her name appears on Handel's scores, but was replaced by another singer (or another movement for a different singer) in every case. The same applies to Handel's second bass, William Savage.

4 Revival and revision, 1743–1759

1 For Handel's coolness towards Smith, see Smith's letter of 28 July 1743, printed in Eisen and Eisen, *Händel-Handbuch*, 4, pp. 363–4.

2 *Ibid.*, p. 363.

3 See Mrs Delany's letters of 10 and 22 March (Deutsch, *Handel*, pp. 587–8). There are no

annotations in the conducting score that could be attributed to a planned performance in 1744.

4 Deutsch, *Handel*, pp. 590–1.

5 *Ibid.*, p. 602.

6 CJ (from Queen's Square) to EH, 28 February 1744/5; see Eisen and Eisen, *Händel-Handbuch*, 4, p. 386.

7 Handel's regular oratorio nights this season were Wednesday and Friday: the special arrangement for Holy Week was presumably motivated by the need to avoid Good Friday.

8 See the table in Burrows, 'The Autographs', p. 219.

9 The evidence for this date is derived from the copyist and the paper type of the insertions in the conducting score.

10 In the process the 'Romans' text for 'How beautiful are the Feet' received performance for the first time. The duet-and-chorus movement to the similar Isaiah text was put out of commission and Handel may never have performed it again. See Burrows, 'The Autographs', pp. 214–15.

11 See pp. 42–3. Other revisions in 1745 may have included minor amendments to the word-underlay in 'He shall feed his flock/Come unto him' and 'If God be for us', which were altered in the conducting score in a handwriting very similar to Jennens's.

12 30 August 1745, from Gopsal. Letter with Jennens–Holdsworth correspondence but no addressee; Jennens repeats, as if for the first time, issues already made familiar to Holdsworth, so a different addressee may be assumed.

13 Paper characteristics suggest that Jennens's score was copied *c*.1744–5, with further amendments *c*.1745–7; his part-books were copied from an independent source *c*.1745–8. See Burrows, 'The Autographs'.

14 Smith, *Handel*, pp. 284, 295. The keyboard version of the overture was not Handel's arrangement: see Terence Best, 'Handel's Overtures for Keyboard', *The Musical Times*, 126 (1985), p. 90.

15 Vol. 5, Part 3 (1744); see Smith, *Handel*, p. 323, and Mrs Dewes's letter of 1750 (Deutsch, *Handel*, p. 695).

16 Letter, CJ to EH 20 January 1745/6.

17 See the table in Burrows, 'The Autographs', p. 219.

18 When the sequence was divided between two voices, each sang two successive movements: Handel never changed the voice at 'But Thou didst not leave'.

19 See Watkins Shaw, 'Covent Garden Performances of "Messiah" in 1749, 1752 and 1753', *The Music Review*, 19 (1958), p. 85.

20 In a couple of places he adapted the music to give the ripieno strings musically sensible entries: his amendments ('And he shall purify', bars 15–16; 'And with his stripes', B and T bars 19–21, S bars 10–11) may have been retained (without the accompanying ripieno directions that caused them) in subsequent years. The Foundling Hospital lists for 1754, 1758 and 1759 show four oboes and four bassoons.

21 See Burrows, 'Handel and the Foundling Hospital'.

22 Smith, *Handel*, pp. 190–1.

23 A strange legacy from the controversy of 1743 seems to have been Walsh's reluctance to name the work: where other arias in the anthology carried the name of the parent oratorio, the *Messiah* arias had a blank space. By 1749 Walsh almost certainly held a copy-text of a complete set of arias from *Messiah*, from which he also set up a collected volume of songs in *Messiah* a couple of years later: but *Songs in Messiah* was temporarily stored and withheld from publication.

24 The 1 May figure is close to the estimated capacity of Covent Garden Theatre. The 15 May figures do not take account of the 'gratis' tickets, whose total number is unknown. See Burrows, 'Handel and the Foundling Hospital', p. 283.

25 The motive for Frasi's withdrawal is not known: since the Hospital performances took place during the daytime, there should have been no conflict with her theatre engagements. Frasi

was always the most expensive soloist in subsequent Foundling Hospital lists. There was an obvious appropriateness in the employment of a boy treble for performances in aid of a children's charity.

26 Deutsch, *Handel*, pp. 751–3. Whether Handel performed as an instrumentalist at any revivals of *Messiah* after 1753 may be doubted. Organ concertos, with Handel as soloist, had been included in performances at Dublin (1742) and London (1743), and at various subsequent revivals. In 1750 Handel naturally 'opened' the organ that he had given to the Foundling Hospital Chapel with some solo music, and his organ playing was recorded as one of the features of his *Messiah* performances there in the next two years. The last newspaper reference to Handel playing the organ in public is in connection with the Hospital's *Messiah* performance on 1 May 1753 (Deutsch, p. 742).

27 General Committee Minutes, 3 May 1758 (not included in Deutsch, *Handel* or Eisen and Eisen, *Händel-Handbuch*, 4). The composer was also thanked for his attendance at the performance.

28 See Deutsch, *Handel*, p. 816.

29 Subcommittee minutes, 2 January 1754: Burrows, 'Handel and the Foundling Hospital', p. 279.

30 Foundling Hospital General Committee Minutes 23 January 1754; for the petition, see Deutsch, *Handel*, pp. 756–7 and Burrows, 'Handel and the Foundling Hospital', pp. 278–9.

31 Deutsch, *Handel*, p. 789.

32 See Burrows, 'Handel and the Foundling Hospital', pp. 279–280, and Smith, *Handel*, pp. 116–17.

33 A case for (occasional) performances of *Messiah* 'as composed' is made in Graydon Beeks, 'Some thoughts on performing "Messiah", *American Choral Review*, 27 (1985), p. 20.

34 The first, deleted, attempt – ending, unusually, with a cadence in the subdominant – is reprinted in John Tobin, *Handel's "Messiah"* (London 1969), p. 57.

35 See, however, Burrows, 'The Autographs', pp. 214–15, for some inconclusive evidence that Handel might have considered reviving the duet-and-chorus setting of 'How beautiful are the feet' for one of his later performances.

36 The original all-soprano version seems to have received but rare performances at his hands: he may first have included it at Covent Garden performances in 1752, and then revived it in 1754 (as reflected in the Foundling Hospital part-books).

37 For the elision of the second melisma, see Burrows, 'The Autographs', which supplements and corrects Burrows, 'Handel's performances'. Smith carried Handel's amendments forward from the autograph to the conducting score, but Handel also worked on the movement in the latter: see his amendment to a detail of the viola part at bar 39, removing relatively insignificant consecutive octaves.

38 The thematic material at bars 85–8 had been anticipated at the beginning of the B section of 'Che bel contento' from *Flavio* (1723), printed *HG* vol. 67, p. 26.

39 See Burrows, 'The Autographs' and 'Handel's Performances'.

40 For a reconstruction of Handel's schemes (for all performances between 1742 and 1754, with the exception of 1745) see the table 'The Alternative Versions of "Messiah"', prefaced to the Burrows edition of the vocal score; the main text of the vocal score gives an eleventh version.

41 The origin of this practice is rather obscure. The first published full score (1767) gave Handel's original bass version 5b/A2/6a, and the later 'Guadagni' aria 5/6i/6 in an appendix. The solo part in the latter was correctly printed in the treble clef, which was otherwise used for soprano, alto and tenor with no distinction, so it would have been possible to misconstrue 'But who may abide' as an aria for tenor. The decisive shift came with Mozart who, working from the printed edition, decided to put the 'Guadagni' version into the bass clef. (He apparently attempted to arrange the original bass aria, before rejecting it in favour

of the 'Guadagni' version: see the Kritischer Bericht to *Neue Mozart Ausgabe* X/28, Abt. 1 Bd. 2, p. 56). The mis-application of the bass voice to this aria in Britain seems to be mostly attributable to the influence of the 'Mozart' version on Vincent Novello, who printed the solo part of the 'Guadagni' version in the bass clef in his vocal score.

5 *Messiah* in other hands

1 See the Earl of Shaftesbury's letter, 20 May 1756, printed Eisen and Eisen, *Händel-Handbuch*, 4, p. 498.
2 See Boydell: *A Dublin Musical Calendar.* The performances were normally given in November or December; there were two performances in 1744, the first (in February) delayed from the previous December.
3 The printed word-book for this performance, dated 16 February 1743 [i.e. with 'old style' year], was closely based on Handel's London 1743 word-book text.
4 See Deutsch, *Handel*, p. 664. The celebrations, which constituted almost a Handel festival, with performances of his works on three days, were conducted by William Hayes, who received his Doctorate from the University in the accompanying degree ceremony.
5 These dates are taken from printed word-books and from the registers of provincial performances in volumes of the *Royal Musical Association Research Chronicle.*
6 The relationship between the music of this score and Hayes's performances is uncertain. His score originated before Handel's 1745 revisions, and therefore preserved an 'old' version of the work that may have been reflected in some of his performances. The 1750 Salisbury performance conducted by Hayes included Guadagni among the soloists, and it is difficult to believe that Guadagni did not then perform the arias that Handel had written especially for him earlier that year.
7 On the Church Langton performances, which must be the first 'village' performances of *Messiah*, see William Hanbury, *The History of the Rise and Progress of the Charitable Foundations at Church-Langton* (London 1767).
8 John Stanley and Felice de' Giardini.
9 The performers' list in Burney, *An Account* includes the names of all those who took part in the five performances. Lists in the programme-books for individual performances vary slightly, but even these seem to be inaccurate for any given occasion. Apart from a few sopranos among the trebles, the chorus was all-male.
10 The new large market for vocal scores, combined with new production methods, reduced the cost of the music dramatically: Vincent Novello's vocal score, issued in 1846 for 6s. 6d (or unbound at 6s.), appeared in a pocket edition in 1859 for 1s. 4d, and soon afterwards came down to 1s.
11 At the Festival of the Sons of the Clergy: see Deutsch, *Handel*, p. 798.
12 The original score did not name these instruments, and Handel may not have used them in Dublin. The chorus 'Their sound is gone out', composed in 1745, included independent oboe lines, and from this it may be inferred that from now on (as also possibly in 1743) Handel employed oboes and bassoons in his performances.
13 It is not clear whether flutes were used for the Commemoration *Messiah* performances (see note 9, *supra*).
14 See Burney, *An Account*, 'Fifth Performance', p. 112. The novelty of the trombones (which may not have been heard or seen in London since 1741) is attested by a contemporary manuscript annotation to a copy of the programme for the First Performance in the Gerald Coke Collection: in the list of performers, against 'Trombones' is written 'Are something like Bassoons, with an end like a large speaking trumpet'.
15 It is sometimes said that Mozart's additional accompaniments were written because there was no organ in the hall where he performed the work, but this seems an unlikely motive: Mozart simply arranged the oratorio according to the regular forces that were available to

him (including horns, flutes and clarinets), and under the influence of prevailing harmonic tastes. He did not score up *semplice* recitatives, which were presumably accompanied by harpsichord.

16 Published in the *Neue Mozart Ausgabe*, X/28, Abt. 1 Bd. 2, ed. Andreas Holschneider (Kassel 1961).

17 Letter from van Swieten to Mozart, 21 March 1789, quoted in the Kritischer Bericht to the *NMA* edition (see note 16), p. 48.

18 See Douglas Johnson, Alan Tyson and Robert Winter, *The Beethoven Sketchbooks* (Oxford 1985), pp. 267, 270, 525.

19 W. G. Cusins, *Handel's Messiah. An Examination of the Original and of some Contemporary MSS* (London 1874). Some of Cusins's conclusions on points of detail now seem misjudged, but he made a serious attempt to grapple with important issues.

20 *The Hornet*, 4 July 1877; *The World*, 21 January 1891. However, in another article (*The Star*, 3 January 1889) Shaw clearly approved of the 'mass appeal' that had been generated for *Messiah* by the conventional large performances.

21 Shaw, *A Textual and Historical Companion*, pp. 89–90.

22 Now in the Rowe Library, King's College, Cambridge.

23 The *Händelgesellschaft* edition score was prepared by Friedrich Chrysander, but he did not live to see it in print: the work was completed by Max Seiffert, who commendably included the soprano/alto variant to the duet-and-chorus version of 'How beautiful are the Feet', which had not been in Chrysander's scheme.

24 'The Earliest Editions of Handel's "Messiah"', *The Musical Times*, 66 (1925), p. 985, later supplemented by a second article (*ibid.* 82 (1941), p. 427), and then republished in a revised version in William C. Smith, *Concerning Handel* (London 1948).

25 Beecham's last *Messiah* recording was made as late as 1959, and Sargent's in 1964. Although 'inauthentic' as to scoring, Beecham's second recording (1947) was the first 'complete' performance on record, appearing first as twenty-one 12-inch 78 r.p.m. records and then re-issued on four long-playing records in the mid-1950s.

26 The London Choral Society chorus had 60–70 singers. I thank Sheila Hills, one of the chorus members who sang in Tobin's performances, for this information.

27 Significant landmarks were the recordings of Colin Davis and Charles Mackerras in 1966–7.

28 See Winton Dean, reviewing the editions of Shaw and Tobin in *The Musical Times*, 108 (1967), p. 157.

29 *Hallische Händel-Ausgabe*, Serie 1 Band 17 (full score and Kritischer Bericht, Kassel 1965); *Handel at Work* (London 1964); *Handel's "Messiah"* (London 1969).

30 Choir of Christ Church Cathedral, Oxford, with The Academy of Ancient Music, directed by Christopher Hogwood.

6 Design

1 *SAMSON, AN ORATORIO. As it is Perform'd at the THEATRE-ROYAL in Covent Garden* (London 1747, first issues).

2 Letter of 30 August 1745; see p. 35.

3 Apart from 'He was despised', all of the solo music in 'scenes' I–IV of Part Two was composed for a tenor-clef soloist.

4 It is noticeable that the more 'secular' works drop from Handel's programmes, *Hercules* by 1752, *Acis and Galatea* and *Semele* by 1742 and 1744 respectively. Even secular works with arguably religious or ethical connections – *Alexander's Feast*, *The Choice of Hercules*, *L'Allegro* and the shorter Cecilian Ode – vanish after 1755.

5 See Anthony Hicks, 'The late additions to Handel's oratorios and the role of the younger Smith', *Music in Eighteenth-Century England*, ed. Christopher Hogwood and Richard Luckett (Cambridge 1983), p. 147.

6 Jennens may possibly have expected more musical emphasis in Part Two/II; the literary proportions nevertheless remain unequal in the first two scenes.

7 Allowance must be made for the fact that Jennens not only combined the texts, but altered the wording of some of them. At the time he assembled the libretto of *Messiah*, the relevance of the prophecies of 'second' Isaiah (*Isaiah* 40 onwards) to the Messiah was a matter of public controversy.

8 See Geoffrey Cuming, 'The Text of "Messiah"', *Music & Letters*, 31 (1950), p. 226.

9 The quotation comes from a late source (John Nichols, *Literary Anecdotes of the Eighteenth Century*, 2nd edn, 1812–15). 'Reading prayers' does not imply any clerical status, from which Jennens would have debarred himself as a non-juror. The period to which the anecdote applies is also uncertain: Jennens did not become master of Gopsal in his own right until 1747, and lived another twenty-six years.

10 For a full discussion of this aspect, see Ruth Smith 'The Achievements'.

11 Preface to the word-book for Handel's performances, *ALEXANDER's FEAST; OR, THE POWER OF MUSICK* [Dryden, adapted Hamilton] (London 1736).

12 After 1745 this scene was preceded by two aria–chorus units, which may perhaps also be interpreted as a 'regularisation' of the scheme in this area.

13 With the exception of *Israel in Egypt* (which has trumpets in C), all of Handel's London oratorios and church music use trumpets in D, thus biasing the keys of the movements in which they are employed.

14 The duets are printed in *Händelgesellschaft* edition (henceforward, *HG*) 32 (second edn, Leipzig 1880); Handel's autographs are in British Library RM 20.g.9.

15 Derived in turn from the cantata with the same text (*c*.1739), HWV 154; autograph in Fitzwilliam Museum, Cambridge Mu. MS 261.

16 Although the occasion or singers for which Handel composed the duets remain obscure, there is no reason to regard the duets as in some way 'sketches' or compositional trials for *Messiah*: they are independent compositions.

17 Handel's subsequent re-settings of the aria were also in this key, but the 'Guadagni' version was variously transposed after 1753 for soprano, into A minor and G minor.

18 This aria and the preceding recitative were also variously performed by Handel in versions transposed to F major, and divided F major/B flat major.

19 Handel's autograph separates the movements by only a single bar-line, accompanied by the new time-signature and *tempo* indication.

20 Whether this implies an application of 'double dots' to the chorus is another matter. Such rhythmic alteration can be made to work in the first section and the orchestral postlude, but is more difficult to apply to the thematic material for 'That taketh away the sin of the world' in bars 19–20, particularly on the word 'away'.

21 Both movements are marked 'Largo' and are surely intended to be taken at the same, or closely-related, speeds: there is no authority from any source for taking the 'B' section of 'He was despised' faster than the remainder.

22 Against this it may be noted that the first repetition of 'Behold' in 'Behold and see' is also a major sixth: but the point at issue concerns the effect of the initial anacruces, and not the compositional continuations. In talking of a 'bright' major sixth (and, previously, of the transition from minor to major as a musical analogue to the transition from crucifixion to resurrection) I am, of course, loading the music with an interpretation that might be regarded as anachronistic, more appropriate to the transition from minor to major keys in, for example, Beethoven's Fifth Symphony. While it would be wrong to suggest that the 'major/minor', 'happy/sad' equation was generally appropriate to Baroque music of the 1740s – consider, for example, Handel's use of major key for the forceful 'Why do the nations' or for the pathos of 'He was despised' – nevertheless in *Messiah* Handel made good use of the emotional effect of a transition between minor and major modes. The 'opening-out' effect between the E minor of the overture and the E major of 'Comfort ye' is a

striking gesture at the beginning of the work. The trick also works in reverse, as the blandly wandering F major of 'All we, like sheep' darkens to F minor at the end as the Messiah bears 'the iniquity of us all'. One fairly obvious place for the employment of minor/major contrast is the chorus 'Since by man came death', a contrast that Handel heightened by the transition from unaccompanied voices to full orchestral-choral *tutti*. It seems rather strange at first sight that, while Handel took the opportunity to make the contrast (A minor–C major) at the first statement, the second statement ('For as in Adam') does not repeat the gambit, proceeding instead from G minor to D minor. Here the expressive opportunities for contrast of mode seem to have taken second place to wider architectural-tonal considerations. Handel wanted to end the chorus in the same key as it started (A minor), and a major key at 'even so in Christ' would have been inconvenient to the scheme: so, for the second statement, the repeated contrast between unaccompanied voices and full ensemble had to suffice. Handel probably felt that the emotional point had been sufficiently made by the first minor–major transition.

7 Individual movements

1 The autographs of the last three are headed 'accomp'; the first page of the autograph of 'Comfort ye' is lost, but Handel's similar heading was directly transcribed into the conducting score.

2 See Winton Dean, *Handel's Dramatic Oratorios and Masques* (London 1959), Appendix A, p. 627.

3 In terms of musical form, there is little significant distinction between these *da capo* arias and those *dal segno* arias (such as 'How beautiful are the Feet' in its first version) that merely elide the opening ritornello at the *reprise*.

4 Shaw and Tobin include the long form of this aria as a *dal segno* in their editions of *Messiah*. It is clear from the autograph, however, that this was originally composed as a full *da capo* aria, returning to bar 1 after a semibreve chord in bar 113: the lead-back bars seem to be a subsequent addition, provided during Handel's revision of the movement into its shorter form (16a/18ii/16ax).

5 These are anticipated in the aria 'Ti vedrò regnar sul trono' from *Riccardo Primo* (1727) and the last movement of the Concerto Grosso, Op. 6, No. 2 (1739) respectively.

6 The path from duet to chorus is continuous, with no speed change: Handel provided a physical link in the basso continuo part at the end of the duet.

7 'O Death, where is thy sting' also begins without an opening orchestral ritornello, but with the 'walking bass' carried over from the Italian Duet original, which establishes the movement's chamber-music-like character.

8 Handel's word setting

1 Some of these idiosyncrasies, particularly 'strenght', were shared by Handel's copyists. Smith senior faithfully copied Handel's erroneous 'death' (for 'dead') several times into the conducting score, where it was altered by a later hand, possibly Jennens's.

2 See Note 29 to the libretto (p. 100). The combined testimony of the 1742 and 1743 word-books suggests that the reading of the text that Handel received from Jennens in 1742 was 'maketh'.

3 Handel usually clarified word-underlay by the grouping of quaver-beams and the employment of syllable-slurs: the latter were frequently necessary where text and music were not in unambiguous vertical alignment. In the original 'long' 12/8 version of 'Rejoice greatly', 'cometh' is clearly treated as a single syllable in three places (bars 34, 81, 83) and may have been intended as two syllables at bars 31, 52 and 65, though Handel's intentions in these places are uncertain because of textual mis-alignment or compositional alterations. In the

common-time version Handel set the word as two syllables except at bar 34, where his conventional signs suggest one syllable (which would indeed solve a practical articulation problem). Handel's single-syllable 'cometh' may have been influenced by the German 'kommt'.

4 Yet other 'solutions' were adopted by early copyists: one manuscript copy from the mid-1760s (British Library RM 18.c.2; copyist S5) has Ex. 10 and Ex. 11. Jennens himself favoured Ex. 11 in his keyboard score (British Library RM 19.d.1): for the first passage, he treated the last chord of the *Pifa* as the first beat of the recitative, and brought the voice in on beat 2 with the rhythm as in Ex. 3(b), p. 76.

Ex. 10 (from RM 18.c.2)

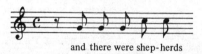

and there were shep-herds

Ex. 11 (from RM 18.c.2.)

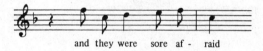

and they were sore af - raid

Ex. 12 another 'solution' by the same copyist, from the 'Lennard' manuscript:

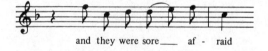

and they were sore____ af - raid

5 As, for example, by David Thomas on the recording conducted by Christopher Hogwood (L'Oiseau-Lyre, 1980).

6 Incontrovertible identification is not possible, but the hand and ink are very similar to those from Jennens's amendments in other Handel scores: a slightly greater heaviness in the pen-stroke may be attributed to the need to cover Handel's original words. The period of the amendments to *Messiah* can be established with some certainty from secondary copies: 'Come unto him' had been altered before the 'Granville' transcript was taken in 1743–4 and 'If God be/is for us' had been changed before 1749. The 'Jennens' hand also converted 'soul' to 'souls' in the conducting score, in 'Come unto him'.

7 The word-books conflict with the conducting score: the 1742 word-book has 'is', that of 1743 (presumably approved by Jennens) has 'be'. Subsequent word-books (1749 onwards) reverted to 'be', even though they seem to have derived most of their texts from the 1742 (rather than 1743) word-book; there is no evidence of any reversion to 'be' in the musical sources.

8 Manchester Central Libraries, Newman Flower Collection MS 130 Hd4 v. 200. See Burrows, 'The Autographs'. For transcriptions see Shaw, *A Textual and Historical Companion*, p. 78 and Tobin, *Handel's "Messiah"*, p. 146.

9 It is not entirely clear from Handel's autograph whether Handel regarded 'First-fruits' as one word or two. 1742 and 1749 word-books have 'first Fruits', 1743 (as also possibly the source text from Jennens) has 'First-Fruits'.

10 The version from the conducting score naturally appears in sources (including Jennens's score and the first printed editions) that were derived directly or indirectly from this source. The 'Goldschmidt' copy, derived from the autograph at this point and thus carrying the alternative reading, was subsequently altered, possibly by one of the Hayes family in the eighteenth century, to another 'editorial' variant, as Ex. 12.

Ex. 12   'Goldschmidt', as amended

the   first - fruits of   them,   of   them___   that   sleep.

11 On this matter, see Burrows, 'The Autographs'.

12 *The Musical Times*, 130 (1989), p. 97; Stanley Sadie, reviewing a Covent Garden production of *Semele*.

Select bibliography

Beeks, Graydon, 'Some Thoughts on Performing "Messiah"', *American Choral Review*, 27, nos. 2–3 (1985), p. 20.

Boydell, Brian, *A Dublin Musical Calendar 1700–1760* (Blackrock 1988).

Burney, Charles, *An Account of the Musical Performances ... in Commemoration of Handel* (London 1785, facsimile reprint Amsterdam 1964).

Burrows, Donald, 'Handel and the Foundling Hospital', *Music & Letters*, 58 (1977), p. 269.

'Handel's Performances of "Messiah": The Evidence of the Conducting Score', *Music & Letters*, 56 (1975), p. 319. See also *Music & Letters*, 58 (1977), p. 121.

'The Autographs and Early Copies of "Messiah": Some Further Thoughts', *Music & Letters*, 66 (1985), p. 201. See also *Music & Letters*, 67 (1986), p. 344.

'Newly-recovered "Messiah" Scores', *Newsletter of the American Handel Society*, 4, no. 3 (1989), pp. 1, 5.

Burrows, Donald and Ronish, Martha, *A Catalogue of Handel's Musical Autographs* (Oxford, forthcoming).

Chrysander, Friedrich (ed.), *Das Autograph des Oratoriums 'Messiah'* (Hamburg 1892, reprinted New York 1969). Facsimile of autograph materials.

Clausen, Hans Dieter, *Händels Direktionspartituren ('Handexemplare')*, Hamburger Beiträge zur Musikwissenschaft, vol. 7 (Hamburg 1972).

Deutsch, Otto Erich, *Handel: A Documentary Biography* (London 1955, reprinted New York 1974). For a further, revised edn see Eisen and Eisen. Texts reprinted in both volumes are given page references only from Deutsch.

Eisen, Walter and Eisen, Margret, *Händel-Handbuch, herausgegeben vom Kuratorium der Georg-Friedrich-Händel-Stiftung von Dr. Walter Eisen and Dr. Margret Eisen*, gleichzeitig Supplement zu Hallische Händel-Ausgabe. Vols. 1–3 (Leipzig 1978, 1984, 1986) contain the *Thematisch-systematisches Verzeichnis* to Handel's works prepared by Professor B. Baselt. Vol. 4 (Leipzig 1985), *Dokumente zu Leben und Schaffen*, is a revised and supplemented version of Deutsch, *Handel: A Documentary Biography*.

Gudger, William D., 'Sketches and Drafts for "Messiah"', *American Choral Review*, 27, nos. 2–3 (1985), p. 31.

Handel's Conducting Score of Messiah, facsimile, with an introduction by Watkins Shaw (London 1974).

Hicks, Anthony, 'Handel, Jennens and "Saul": Aspects of a Collaboration' in *Music and Theatre, Essays in honour of Winton Dean*, ed. Nigel Fortune (Cambridge 1987), p. 203.

Larsen, Jens Peter, *Handel's 'Messiah': Origins, Composition, Sources* (London 1957, second edn with additions and minor revisions New York 1972).

[Mainwaring, John], published anonymously, *Memoirs of the Life of the Late George Frederic Handel* (London 1760, facsimile reprint Buren 1964, 1975).

(Sacred Harmonic Society), *Facsimile of the Autograph Score of Messiah* (London 1868).

Sadie, Stanley and Hicks, Anthony (eds.), *Handel Tercentenary Collection* (London 1987).

Shaw, Watkins, *A Textual and Historical Companion to Handel's 'Messiah'* (London 1965).

A First List of Word-books of Handel's 'Messiah', 1742–1783 (Worcester 1959).

Handel's Conducting Score of 'Messiah' (Tenbury Wells 1962).

Smith, Ruth, 'The Achievements of Charles Jennens (1700–1773)', *Music & Letters*, 70 (1989), p. 161.

Smith, William C., *Handel. A Descriptive Catalogue of the Early Editions* (London 1960, second edn. Oxford 1970).

Towe, Teri Noel, '"Messiah": Reduplication without Redundancy – Editions and Recordings past and present', *The American Organist*, 19, no. 2 (1985), p. 74.

Index

Index

Index